A note on BLACKWATER

Michael McDowell has taken on a
remarkable challenge with a novel the scope
of BLACKWATER.

His work has ranged from the contemporary
novel of horror set in the American South
(THE AMULET, COLD MOON OVER
BABYLON, and THE ELEMENTALS) to the
extravagantly detailed novel of America in
another time (GILDED NEEDLES and
KATIE).

His fullest powers are mustered now in his
six-part novel BLACKWATER, which Peter
Straub, author of GHOST STORY, says
"looks like Michael McDowell's best yet...it
seduces and intrigues...makes us impatient
for the next volume." Straub says McDowell
is "beyond any trace of doubt, one of the
absolutely best writers of horror"; Stephen
King calls McDowell "the finest writer of
paperback originals in America"; and the
Washington Post promises "Cliffhangers
guaranteed."

*Other Avon Books in the
Blackwater Series by*
Michael McDowell

THE FLOOD
THE LEVEE
THE HOUSE

Coming Soon
THE FORTUNE
RAIN

Other Avon Books by
Michael McDowell
THE AMULET
COLD MOON OVER BABYLON
THE ELEMENTALS
GILDED NEEDLES
KATIE

MICHAEL McDOWELL'S

BLACKWATER: IV

THE WAR

◆ AVON
PUBLISHERS OF BARD, CAMELOT, DISCUS AND FLARE BOOKS

BLACKWATER: IV THE WAR is an original publication of Avon Books. This work has never before appeared in book form.

Front cover illustration by Wayne D. Barlowe

AVON BOOKS
A division of
The Hearst Corporation
959 Eighth Avenue
New York, New York 10019

First Avon Printing, April, 1983

AVON TRADEMARK REG. U. S. PAT. OFF. AND IN OTHER COUNTRIES. MARCA REGISTRADA. HECHO EN U. S. A.

Printed in the U. S. A.

WFH 10 9 8 7 6 5 4 3 2 1

BLACKWATER: IV

THE WAR

Our story 'til now ...

In THE HOUSE, Volume III of the BLACKWATER saga, the Caskey sisters, Miriam and Frances, grow up as virtual strangers to each other. Miriam, spoiled and imperious, lives with her grandmother Mary-Love in the house next door to Frances and their parents, Elinor and Oscar. Frances, her mother's darling, is a timid and fearful child, afraid most of all of the very house in which she lives, and the strange presences she is certain inhabit it. Always sickly, she falls seriously ill after an expedition to the source of her mother's beloved Perdido River, and is confined to her bed for three years, where she is bathed twice daily by Elinor in Perdido water until she recovers.

Queenie Strickland, sister-in-law to the widowed James Caskey, peacefully raises her children Lucille, Malcolm and Danjo until her husband Carl returns and resumes his violent attacks. After his almost murderous spree against Queenie and against her own home, Elinor sees to it that Carl meets a grisly end in the Perdido.

Elinor's mother-in-law, Mary-Love, also meets an untimely end, and though she dies in her bed, she has the curious sensation during her last days that she is being slowly filled and drowned by the waters of the Perdido. After Mary-Love's death, Elinor becomes head of the Caskey family and its considerable fortune, which she will administer more generously and justly than Mary-Love ever did.

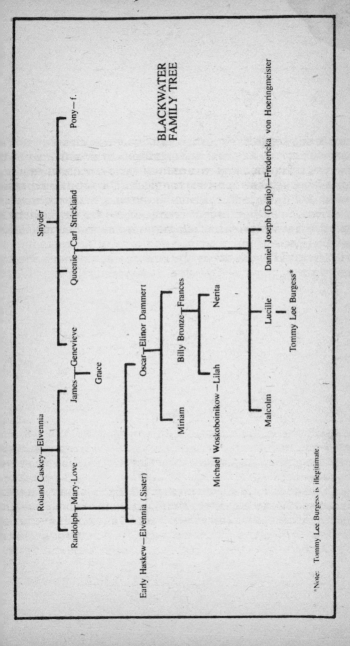

BLACKWATER
FAMILY TREE

Snyder — Pony — f.

Roland Caskey — Elvennia

James — Genevieve

Grace

Queenie — Carl Strickland

Oscar — Elinor Dammert

Randolph — Mary-Love

Early Haskew — Elvennia (Sister)

Miriam

Billy Bronze — Frances

Michael Woskoboinikow — Lilah

Nerita

Malcolm

Lucille

Tommy Lee Burgess*

Daniel Joseph (Danjo) — Fredericka von Hoeringmeister

*Note: Tommy Lee Burgess is illegitimate.

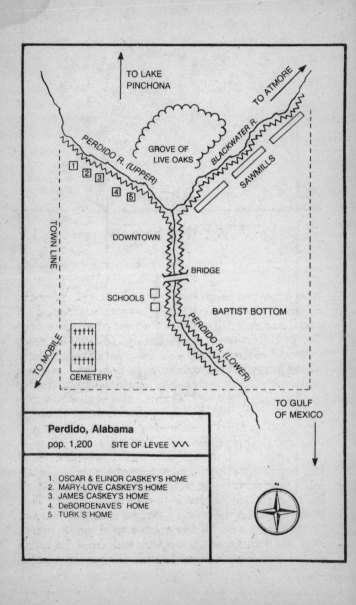

TO LAKE
PINCHONA

TO ATMORE

PERDIDO R. (UPPER)

BLACKWATER R.

GROVE OF
LIVE OAKS

SAWMILLS

1
2
3
4
5

TOWN LINE

DOWNTOWN

BRIDGE

SCHOOLS

BAPTIST BOTTOM

TO MOBILE

PERDIDO R. (LOWER)

CEMETERY

TO GULF
OF MEXICO

N

Perdido, Alabama

pop. 1,200   SITE OF LEVEE ∿∿

1. OSCAR & ELINOR CASKEY'S HOME
2. MARY-LOVE CASKEY'S HOME
3. JAMES CASKEY'S HOME
4. DeBORDENAVE'S HOME
5. TURK'S HOME

CHAPTER 43

At the Beach

Mary-Love had been dead for two years. In the months following the funeral, the Caskeys were watchful for shifts and transformations that were bound to happen in the makeup of the family. Alterations were slow and subtle. Elinor and Oscar and Frances were little changed, although Elinor's demeanor seemed easier now that her chief rival and enemy had finally been defeated in death. Frances was sixteen, a sophomore in high school, and the three years that she had spent in a bed of arthritic pain were distant and dim and only occasionally disquieting.

Next door, Sister Haskew had not gone back to her husband, who dutifully turned up each Christmas, and perhaps once or twice in between. With every visit he and his wife seemed more distant. This break between them had never been acknowledged. Sister would say, "Early travels so doggone much. How am I supposed to keep up with him? I'd much rather stay here in Perdido with Miriam, who needs me." The last part of this statement wasn't quite true, for Miriam—at eighteen—considered that she needed no one. She saw herself as her grandmother's true heir. More important than her grandmother's money and bonds and stock, which had been divided equally between Sister and Oscar, Miriam had inherited Mary-Love's house and—filial considerations notwithstanding—she had been endowed with Mary-Love's enmity toward Elinor Caskey. Miriam would not speak to her mother when they passed on the street, or wave when they saw each other out of the windows of their houses. Miriam would nod grudgingly to her father Oscar, and never lacked a cruel word for her sister Frances, whom she encountered frequently in school.

Sister and her strong-willed niece Miriam formed an unhappy household, always on edge, cringing beneath the lowering cloud of their individual secrets. Sister would not admit, even to Miriam, that she no longer loved her husband—that indeed she dreaded even his infrequent brief visits. Miriam would not declare open hostility toward her mother for fear that she would somehow be crushed by Elinor's superior knowledge of strategy and experience in combat.

In the house next door in the other direction, James Caskey had turned into an old man. Yet he was supremely happy in raising his nephew Danjo, now fourteen. Danjo loved James and never did anything that angered or disappointed his uncle. On the other hand, Danjo's older brother and sister—Malcolm and Lucille—were problems to Danjo's mother, Queenie Strickland. Malcolm was twenty and didn't seem able to do much of anything. He had once got a job in Cantonement, but had lost it after only a week. Another job down in Pensacola lasted even less time. When he returned to his mother in Perdido, Malcolm begged Queenie to find him a place at the lumber

12

mill. Now Malcolm was in charge of a chipper, but due to his inattention was in constant danger of losing one arm or both in the claws of that great, explosive machine. At eighteen, Lucille still simpered and whined, but had grown pretty in a pasty sort of way. She exhibited her modest charms behind the candy counter in the Ben Franklin store and came home every day smelling of rancid popcorn oil. Both Lucille and Malcolm were concerned about the fact that they bore such menial positions. They were, after all, part of the all-powerful Caskey clan.

By owning the only industry in town, the Caskeys might have been considered to own the town itself. They didn't live as if this were the case, however. In delicate consideration of the straitened circumstances of those around them in Perdido, the Caskeys did not display the wealth they assuredly had accumulated. The worst part of the Depression was over, and they had come through it. To survive was to have done well, particularly in this distressed part of the country. The Turk and DeBordenave lumber mills, in operation for decades, had been shut down, and their machinery, land, and employees had been absorbed by the expanding Caskeys. After Mary-Love's death James had turned over the entire operation of the mill to his nephew Oscar. James no longer went to his office, but simply sat out on his porch all day long with his sister-in-law Queenie.

Oscar had played a close game with the mills in the past few years, taking careful advantage of the small opportunities that occasionally came his way. Every penny of the money he made was put back into the mills for expansion, modernization, or acquisition of forested land. By 1938, the Caskeys were rich in their holdings. Yet the mill, the window-and-sash plant, and the factory for the production of fence posts, utility poles, and railroad ties—all in peak condition and possibly the most technologically advanced in the country—were operating at perhaps no more than a quarter of their capacity. Workers frequently were sent home at noon, but received a full day's pay. The Caskeys now owned nearly a third of a million acres of forest in five Alabama and Florida counties, but cutters never had to venture farther than five miles from town because orders were so few. Sister and James needed but little money to live on, for their lives were quiet. Yet even for that little they were forced to go to Oscar, who gave them what they needed in cash of small denominations. This arrangement seemed strange to Sister and James, for the Caskey households had never been restricted in such a manner. James finally asked Oscar if he was sure that he was pursuing the right course with their money and their mill holdings, to which Oscar replied, "Every penny is invested."

Sister said: "I know that, Oscar, but shouldn't we have a little in reserve?"

"We cain't afford to right now," replied Oscar. "We've got to make sure that when this country is on its feet again, we're right up there and ready to get going too."

"Oscar," said James firmly, "this country's been down for almost ten years. What you think's gone get it back up again? Now, I'm not worried for my sake, 'cause I know I can always get along. I just want to make sure that everything's gone be all right for Elinor and Frances and Sister and Miriam. What would happen to Danjo and Queenie and her children if anything happened to me?"

"Don't y'all trust me?" cried Oscar. "Don't y'all know what I'm trying to do?"

"No," said Sister. "I don't think James and I *do* know."

"*I* don't," agreed James.

"I'm trying to make us rich," Oscar announced.

"What for?" asked Sister. "Five years ago, when

things were so bad for everybody, we had all the money in the world anybody could possibly want that was in his right mind. Now you say we're doing all right, but when I want to send Ivey out for a bottle of milk I've got to go over to the mill and break into petty cash."

"That's just for the time being," said Oscar. "And you know it's not that bad, Sister."

"What if it all goes bust?" asked James. "What do we do then?"

"It's not all gone go bust. Y'all just leave me alone for a little while and let me work this thing through. Y'all don't see it, but we're in a very good position."

James and Sister *didn't* see it, but with some misgivings they decided to trust Oscar. "After all," James pointed out to Sister later, "what else can we do?"

If James and Sister had their doubts and gave Oscar no support in matters pertaining to the running of the Caskey mill, Oscar could always count on the trust and confidence of his wife. Elinor invariably said, "Oscar, I know you, and I know you're doing it right."

All the Caskeys attended the ceremonies marking the end of Miriam's high school career. They had discovered from the *Perdido Standard* that Miriam had attained valedictory status in her graduating class. She had said nothing of this, as if in an attempt to deny her family the pleasure of pride in her accomplishment. In her speech, faultlessly delivered, Miriam likened life to a nest of Chinese boxes, and mystified everyone. After the presentation of the graduation certificates, Miriam allowed herself to be kissed by everyone—even her mother, father, and sister. Miriam understood that on such an occasion she must submit to formalized indignities. The afternoon was brutally hot, and the high school seniors, in white gowns and tasseled mortarboards, wandered aimlessly over the football field with their families, as if all had been afflicted with heat fever. Oscar remarked to his daughter, as if he might have been speaking to one of Miriam's classmates whom he had never met, "You think you might be going on to college?"

Miriam paused before answering. "I'm thinking of it," she said at last.

"Where are you thinking of?" asked Elinor, taking advantage of the occasion to speak to her daughter directly and to the point.

"I'm not sure," replied Miriam hastily, glancing around and then running off to hug a detested classmate.

Sister later asked Miriam the same question, but not even she got a straight answer. James said to Sister, "We're not gone find out until the day Miriam takes off—if she does decide to do it."

Sister sighed and said, "Why you suppose Miriam is like that?"

James replied in surprise: "Because of Mary-Love, of course. Haven't you noticed, Sister? Miriam is just like your mama."

And so she was, laying her plans carefully and in secret.

The hot, high summer came on, and still no one knew what was to become of Miriam in the fall. This was a question of no small moment to Sister, for if Miriam went away to school, Sister would have no ostensible reason to remain in Perdido. She would have to think up another excuse for not returning to her husband. And it was nearly inconceivable that Miriam would *not* go to college—a girl who was smart enough to have been valedictorian of her class, with as much social position and as assured a financial future as Miriam was blessed with, was bound for higher education. Sister grew so demoralized by the task of figuring out some way of not having to go back to Early Haskew that she self-indulgently talked herself into believing that Miriam would never go away at all.

So everyone waited impatiently for fall, to see what Miriam would do. But Miriam had an intermediate surprise. One day toward the end of June Miriam attended a party at the casino on Santa Rosa Island, across the bay from Pensacola. From that day forth, she was obsessed with the beach. Every day she departed at five-thirty in the morning in the little roadster she had been given by Mary-Love. She returned in time for the afternoon meal. Her skin grew darker and darker.

"Is she meeting a boy, you think?" Queenie asked James.

"I wonder," said James, and that night asked Sister the same question.

"Are you seeing a boy down at Pensacola Beach?" Sister asked Miriam the following noon when Miriam walked in the house with a towel over her shoulder.

Miriam seemed offended by the question. "Sister, I drive down there and I lie on the beach and soak up the sun."

"I was just wondering," said Sister.

That afternoon, wearing a white sundress that showed off her deep tan to startling effect, Miriam marched across the sandy yard and knocked on the door of her mother's house. Elinor came to the door.

"Elinor, is Frances around?" Miriam asked stiffly. She had hoped that Frances herself or perhaps Zaddie would answer the door. It irked Miriam to speak to her mother.

"No, she's not. She went downtown, but she ought to be back soon. You want to come in and wait?"

"No, ma'am, but when she gets back, would you tell her to come over and see me for a minute? I want

17

to ask her a question." Miriam turned around and marched off before Elinor could say another word.

Frances was startled and alarmed by the summons from her sister, and she hurried next door to deal with the matter as quickly as possible, as a condemned criminal may urge that the time of execution be moved forward rather than put off. Miriam was reading a magazine by the window in her room upstairs.

"Miriam, Mama said you wanted to speak to me." Frances stood in the doorway of the room; Miriam did not encourage her to venture farther in.

"I did. I wanted to know if you wanted to go down to Pensacola with me tomorrow."

With the revelation of the reason for the summons, Frances's amazement only increased. "What . . . what for?" she stammered.

"To lie down on the beach."

Frances stared at Miriam almost as if in a stupor.

"Well," said Miriam impatiently. "Do you want to go or not?"

"Yes," blurted Frances.

"Can you be ready at five-thirty?"

Frances nodded.

"That's when I leave. If you're not out on your porch, I'll leave without you. I'm not gone be going up to Elinor's door and knocking at that hour of the morning, and I'm not gone call out to you, either. Are you gone be out on the front porch when I'm ready to leave?"

Frances nodded again.

"Good," said Miriam. "Ivey'll fix us something to take along, so don't worry about something to eat. If you're gone want to buy things at the concession stand, then you'd better bring a little money."

"All right," returned Frances, lingering hesitantly for further instructions.

18

None came. After a few moments, Miriam looked up and remarked, "Well, why don't you go away now? I'm busy."

In a daze, Frances wandered home. Neither her father nor her mother could interpret the significance of the invitation. Elinor called James to see if he or Queenie had any ideas about what it portended. They couldn't figure it out, and James called Sister. Sister didn't know for sure, but she had an idea: "Maybe Miriam wants everybody to know that she's not going down to Pensacola every day to meet a boy. That could be why she's taking Frances along."

Miriam drove fast. The top of the roadster was down, and the wind was so loud that the sisters were unable to talk to each other. The sun was still low in the sky at that hour of the morning. Miriam and Frances wore bathing suits under their sundresses. The ride took only slightly more than an hour, and when the sisters got to the beach it was still empty. The casino hadn't opened yet, but half a dozen fishermen had cast their lines from the end of the pier. Miriam walked a few hundred yards or so beyond the pier to a stretch of deserted sand and laid out her blanket. She silently pointed to where Frances should spread hers.

"Did you bring any lotion?" asked Miriam abruptly.

"No," said Frances. "Should I have?"

"Of course. You're going to burn anyway because you're not used to the sun, but without lotion you're going to be in horrible pain by the time we get home. Here, use some of mine."

Frances meekly submitted to being doused with the cold lotion. Miriam brusquely rubbed it in, and when she was finished with Frances, performed the same operation on herself.

"What do I do now?" asked Frances timidly.

"Nothing. Just switch sides every once in a while. And don't talk."

When Miriam lay on her stomach, tanning her back, she read. When she lay on her back, she closed her eyes and slept, or at least appeared to sleep.

Frances had never been so bored in her life, not even when she had been confined to her bed with arthritis. She hadn't brought anything to read. Her head was filled with the dull roar of the Gulf of Mexico. Sand fleas jumped onto her legs and bit them. The blindingly white sand and the washed-out sky bleached all color from the landscape, until everything seemed overwhelmingly pale and overwhelmingly bright, like the continual flash of a news camera. She could feel her skin beginning to burn. She dared not speak to her sister, who had peremptorily prohibited conversation.

Frances sat up on the blanket and began to look longingly at the water. At last, when she felt as if her skin were frying and the blood simmering in her arteries, she turned to Miriam and said, "Can I go in?"

"Go in where?" snapped Miriam.

"Go in the water?"

"Yes. Though I don't know why you'd want to. I hate swimming. Watch out for jellyfish. Be careful of the undertow. Somebody saw a shark out there on Wednesday."

"I'll be careful," said Frances, getting up from the towel.

She raced toward the water, and leaped into a wave just then crashing against the shore. The water was deliciously cool and she loved the motion of the waves. She even liked the taste of the salt. Frances had never been in the Gulf before. When she thought of water and bodies of water, she thought only of the muddy Perdido. The Perdido's voice was low, secretive, and made up of a hundred smaller noises, in-

cessant and unidentifiable. The Gulf, on the other
hand, had but a single voice, regular, loud, insistent.
The Perdido's water was dark and murky, as if it
purposely hid things in its depths; the Gulf water
was bright and blue and white, and Frances could
see her feet through it. The bed of the Perdido was
a fathomless sheet of soft black mud in which dead
things were concealed; underneath these crashing
waves lay hard-packed white sand and millions of
fragments of colored shells. Only an occasional sullen bream or catfish swam in the Perdido; here were
clams gaping in the sand, bright clean seaweed, vast
schools of minnows, and larger fish that sometimes
flew cleanly out of the top of a wave.

Frances swam farther out where the fish were
even larger. They moved lazily away at her intrusion. She perceived the undertow Miriam warned her
against, yet somehow she did not feel she was in any
danger. She let herself be pulled out farther. She
now saw that the pier was no more than a dark line
jutting into the water, and her sister was not visible
at all. She realized that she was probably too far out,
but still she was undisturbed. As she lazily swam
back in toward shore she realized she had never been
less than fully confident of her ability to do so.

"I thought you had drowned," said Miriam calmly,
looking up from her book as Frances once again stood
by her towel on the beach, dripping wet. "I looked
up and you had disappeared. You must have gone
out too far."

"No, no..."

"It's time to go home."

Frances glanced at her sister, puzzled. "It cain't
be time to go home yet. We just got here."

Miriam looked up, shading her eyes. "How long
do you think you were out in the water?"

"Twenty minutes? Half an hour?"

Miriam pointed up into the sky. "Look at the sun,"

21

she said. "Straight overhead. It's almost noon. You were in the water for over three hours!"

Frances looked up into the sky, then turned and gazed once more into the warm blue waters of the Gulf of Mexico.

Miriam was silent on the drive home, but Frances didn't mind. Miriam steered with one hand on the wheel and stared pensively at the road through her dark glasses. Frances lay with her head back, limp but not exhausted. As they neared Perdido, Frances tried to think of a way to thank her sister for the surprising invitation, an invitation that had unexpectedly provided a mysteriously important event for her. When they pulled up before Miriam's house, however, Frances had not yet found the courage to speak.

They got out of the car. "Thank you," said Frances meekly, troubled by the inadequacy of her words.

"You better go buy you some lotion this afternoon," said Miriam. "I cain't keep on letting you use mine."

Frances stopped dead in her tracks and considered this. "You mean we're going back tomorrow?" she asked cautiously.

"I go every day," said Miriam, not quite answering the question.

"And you're inviting me to go again?"

Miriam wouldn't go so far as to admit that. "I leave at five-thirty every morning, and there's room in the car. But I never wait for anybody."

Frances grinned and ran home. She told her astonished parents about the morning.

"Are you going again?" her father asked.

"Of course!" cried Frances. "I had a wonderful time!"

"You're burned, darling!" said Elinor. "When you're down there, I want you to spend all your time

22

in the water. That way the sun won't be so bad on your skin!"

"Oh, Mama! I love that water so much! I can hardly wait till tomorrow!"

Elinor Caskey seemed to take particular delight in this announcement, and for weeks thereafter was not heard to speak a word against Miriam, who had provided Frances with a way that she could swim in the Gulf every day.

The pattern for the entire summer was set that first trip. Every sunny morning of the week Miriam and Frances drove down to Pensacola beach. Miriam rarely spoke to her sister, other than to say, "Are you ready?" or "Did you bring money for the toll bridge?" Miriam lay on her blanket, reading, napping, her skin growing ever darker and darker. Frances swam in the Gulf, sometimes breasting the waves, sometimes swimming in the calm water yards below the surface, sometimes lazily allowing herself to be dragged along by the undertow. Once she discovered herself so far out that a school of leaping porpoises passed around her. She threw her arms about one of the smaller ones and was pulled through the water for several miles at a pace faster than any she had ever known before. Another time she dived deep into the water in order to avoid being seen by the workers on a passing shrimp boat, and she narrowly escaped being caught in their trawling nets. When the boat was gone, Frances wondered why she had deliberately and instinctively avoided being seen. Then she realized that to be discovered so far from the beach would excite suspicion. The fishermen would not believe that a sixteen-year-old girl was not in danger bobbing in the water five miles from shore.

Something about the hours spent in the Gulf reminded Frances of the time of her sickness, and of even more vague and distant times before that. She seemed to lose consciousness the minute she breasted the first wave of the morning—or rather she seemed to lose her identity as Frances Caskey. She became someone—or something—else. She could swim from before seven o'clock when she and Miriam arrived at the beach, until eleven, without touching bottom, without feeling fatigue or fear of undertow, sharks, jellyfish, cramps, or loss of direction. When it was time to come in, she did not say to herself, *Miriam is getting ready to go.* Rather, she simply found herself walking up through the waves and onto the beach. Ths sensation was akin to her recollection of the baths her mother had given her during the course of her illness three years earlier. Frances remembered nothing about them except the moment that her mother took her beneath the arms and lifted her from the water. In that motion her identity, temporarily lost in the water, had come back to her. Rising through the breaking surf, feeling the sand and bits of shell beneath her feet, Frances's old identity returned to her, and she forgot all that she had felt and experienced so far from the shore.

Miriam always made some remark to Frances that went something like: "I looked up for you once or twice, but I could never see you. Sometime I'm going to tell Oscar how far out you go. One day you're going to drown, and everybody's going to blame *me.*"

On the always wordless drive back to Perdido Frances tried to remember exactly how she had spent those hours in the water; tried to recall how far out she had gone, how deep she had dived, what fish she had seen. But the sun beat against her eyelids, and she could fetch back nothing more than a vague impression of having plunged so deep that the sunlight produced only a dim sea-green radiance. Or she could summon up only a hazy recollection of having sat cross-legged on the undulating sandy bottom four miles out, or of having stalked and devoured sea

24

trout and crabs that came temptingly near her. All these things were dreams, doubtless, for how could they have been real? Though Frances had spent four hours in the water, and had had no breakfast, she was never the least bit hungry when she trod up the sand toward the blanket on which Miriam lay sunning. At home her father urged her to eat just a little dinner, but her mother always said, "If Frances says she's full, then we ought to leave her alone, Oscar. When she wants food, I guess she knows where to find it."

CHAPTER 44

Creosote

One cloudless pink dawn in September 1938, Frances Caskey was sitting on the front porch of her family's house with her towel draped over her shoulder and a bathing suit on under her dress, waiting for Miriam to emerge from the house next door. No one in the family had been able to determine just why Miriam took Frances to the beach with her every day. It might have been to allay any suspicion that she was meeting a boy in Pensacola, it might have been that Miriam was surreptitiously glad of her sister's company, but whatever the reason Frances was happy to be taken along. On this particular morning, however, Frances waited but Miriam did not come. Although the two sisters had gone to the beach nearly every day for the past two months, they had spoken little, and Frances did not feel assured enough of their relationship to be able to knock on Miriam's door.

Elinor was surprised to find her daughter still

sitting on the porch when she came down to breakfast about an hour or so later.

"What happened to Miriam?" Frances's mother asked.

"I don't know. Do you think she's sick?"

"I'll send Zaddie over to speak to Ivey," said Elinor. "Ivey'll know."

Zaddie returned in a few minutes with alarming news. "Miss Miriam packing up! Miss Miriam going away for good!"

At the moment this information was delivered, there was the sound of a door slamming, and Frances, Elinor, and Ivey turned in time to see Miriam with two suitcases marching out the front door and down the sidewalk toward her roadster. Frances, bewildered, called out to her sister, "I guess we're not going to Pensacola this morning."

"I guess we're not," returned Miriam. "Do I look like I'm dressed for the beach?" She wore a white dress buttoned up the front and low-heeled red shoes. "Do I usually carry suitcases to Santa Rosa?"

"No," said Frances. "Where are you going?"

Miriam had already turned back toward the house. She spoke over her shoulder: "I'm going to college!"

No one had anticipated it. Not even Sister had an inkling of Miriam's plans. Sister stood nervously on the front porch with a cup of coffee, watching as Miriam, now being assisted by Bray, carried bags and packages out to the car. James Caskey came out onto his porch, having sensed that something was up. Sister called over to him, "Miriam's going off to college this morning!"

"No!" cried James Caskey. "Where's she going?"

At that moment Miriam emerged with three hatboxes.

Sister replied to James pointedly, "I don't know. She hasn't told us yet where she's going."

All three Caskey households watched Miriam's

28

roadster fill up with boxes and suitcases. Frances had gone to her room and changed out of her bathing suit and was now once again on the porch. Danjo phoned Queenie, who arrived in haste. When finally the roadster would hold no more, Miriam turned at the end of the sidewalk and faced her assembled family.

"If y'all must know, I'm enrolling this morning at Sacred Heart in Mobile."

"But that's a *Catholic* school," ejaculated Queenie.

"I'm converting," snapped Miriam, climbing into the roadster. She started the engine, put the car in gear, and without further word pulled away from the curb. As she was turning the corner, she waved her hand once in an offhanded and general farewell to the open-mouthed Caskeys.

Everyone was stunned, particularly Sister. They had become so accustomed to Miriam's daily trips to the beach and to her ever-deepening tan that they had forgotten all about the question of whether or not she was to go to college. Now, however, they agreed that it had been very much in character for Miriam to have done it the way she did.

"That girl," said Elinor, "had rather slit her throat than tell you the time of day."

"Here are the keys to the car," said Oscar to his daughter. "You go on down to the beach alone."

Frances shook her head. "It wouldn't be the same."

Though the dust raised by Miriam's roadster still lingered in the air above the road, Frances already missed her sister. The weeks of driving together to and from Pensacola Beach had convinced Frances that her sister's taciturnity, her impatience, her curt manner of speaking were only part of Miriam's essential character.

After breakfast, Oscar went over and visited Sister. They sat on the side porch in the swing. "I suppose this was as much of a surprise to you as it was to the rest of us," Oscar said.

"It was," said Sister desolately. "I always wondered why Miriam would never let me pick up the mail at the post office, why she always insisted on going by herself. It must have been because she didn't want me to see any letters that were coming to her from Sacred Heart."

"I don't think I know anybody who ever went there," said Oscar. "Why you suppose she picked *that* school?"

Sister shrugged. "Oscar, I long time ago gave up trying to figure out why Miriam said or did anything at all. I love her, but I don't understand her."

"She sure is like Mama," said Oscar, shaking his head.

"Except she's young," Sister pointed out, "so it's worse."

"What are you gone do?"

Sister glanced quickly at her brother. "What do you mean?"

"Now that Miriam's gone. Now that you don't have to stay here and take care of her anymore—not that Miriam ever *needed* much taking care of. You going back to Early? Where *is* he these days, anyway?"

"Ohio," said Sister vaguely. "Or Kentucky. Or somewhere."

"You going back up to Nashville?"

"Oh, I thought I'd stay around here for a little while. I'm sure Miriam forgot something or other and is gone want it sent down. I guess I better wait around to see what it is."

"Elinor could do that if you wanted to get on back to Early."

Sister didn't reply.

"Well?" said Oscar after a few moments.

"Oscar," said Sister, rising in haste, "you stop going on about this, you hear? You let me do what I want!"

30

"All right," said Oscar, confused and abashed by his sister's vehemence. "I just thought—"

"You thought wrong," said Sister in a low voice. "This house belongs to Miriam, and she said I could stay on as long as I wanted. I would appreciate it if you would not come over here early in the morning and try to sweep me out of it!"

"Sit down, Sister. I didn't mean to get you upset."

Sister sat down again, but crossed her legs, put her elbow on her knee, and cradled one cheek in her turned-up hand. She was the very picture of a southern spinster of the patrician variety—tall, slender, with prematurely wrinkling parchment skin that was powdered with the scent of roses. When not pinched in a scowl, the intrinsically fine features of her face drooped. Although her expression lacked both robustness and determination, she very much resembled her dead mother. Mary-Love would have been proud. This lack of strength was the result of all the years of Mary-Love's taunts and slights and domination.

"Sister," said Oscar softly, "see, I just didn't know you were having trouble with Early..."

Sister sighed. "It's not trouble, Oscar. It's just that I don't particularly care to go back to him right now." Oscar said nothing, and Sister continued tentatively, "Early travels, he's always on the road. So many places are raising up levees, you'd think the whole world was in danger of flooding. Or maybe it's just that there's somebody up in the CCC that likes Early a whole lot, and gives him work. I don't want to go with him to all those old places."

"What about your house in Nashville?"

"I'd be all alone there! That's not my home—*this* is my home. If I'm gone be all alone, then I might as well be here in Perdido. You and Elinor hate having me next door, is that it?"

"That is not it and you know it. We just want you to be happy."

"Then I'm happy right here, and I'd appreciate it if you would speak one word to everybody concerned, Oscar. Say I do not want to leave this house unoccupied. Say I don't know what would become of Ivey if I went away. Say I am providing a place for Miriam to come home to on her holidays. Say anything you want. Just don't let people keep coming up to me the way you just did, and saying, 'Sister, I know Early's gone be glad to see you...'"

Oscar promised to ease his sister's way.

A card arrived two days later with Miriam's address on it, but nothing else. Both Sister and Frances wrote to her immediately to say how much she was missed. For the next two weeks they hoped for a reply, but no response to their bashfully tender letters was forthcoming. They did not write again.

Sister was seeing what it was like, for the first time in her life, to live alone. The only really difficult time was in the early evening after Ivey had gone home to Bray in Baptist Bottom. Sister ate her supper alone, and sat on the porch and sewed or looked at magazines. At these lonely times, she didn't miss Miriam so much as she missed her mother. Sister was forty-six, but she felt a lot older. She was married, but she thought of herself as an old maid. One morning she said to Ivey, "Ivey, does your daddy still raise bird dogs?"

"Yes, ma'am."

"Then I think I'm gone go out and get me one." She did just that, and having had experience with Early's pit bulls, she was able to wean the puppy successfully herself. She loved the dog very much and called it Grip. Grip eased Sister's loneliness, though Ivey had dire predictions regarding a bird dog not brought up to hunt.

*   *   *

Queenie quit work at the Caskey mills when James
gave up his office there. Her salary, however, continued to be paid out of her brother-in-law's pocket.
In exchange for this support—though the bargain
was never formally struck between them—Queenie
became more than ever a steadfast and indefatigable
companion to James. James and Queenie sat on his
front porch in the morning, and drove around town
in the afternoon. Sometimes they drove down to Pensacola or Mobile for lunch or else went shopping
together; James liked to buy clothes as much as
Queenie did. Some days were devoted to his wardrobe, other days to hers. Queenie and James were so
intimate that without hesitation Queenie could admit, "James, when I first came to this town—when
was it, 1922 I guess—I put it in my head that I was
gone get rid of Carl and marry you, 'cause you were
a rich widower." She laughed the old shrill laugh
that had become dear to him.

James laughed too. "Queenie, you were barking
up the wrong tree. I was an old man even then, and
I never *was* cut out for marriage. My daddy always
used to say I had the 'stamp of femininity' on me,
and I wasn't ever gone be any use to anybody—man,
woman, or child."

"Your daddy was wrong! That was a terrible thing
to say to you."

James Caskey shrugged. "Carl's dead," he said.
"You want me to marry you now?"

"You're too old, James Caskey."

"I'm sixty-eight."

"That's too *old*," squealed Queenie. "I'm only forty-
eight, that's just two years older than Sister. I'm gone
go out and look for me a *young* man..."

In such merry chafing they passed their days and
evenings together. And if either had problems or
difficulties they never hesitated to confide in each

other. Just at this time, Queenie's principal difficulty was with her son Malcolm.

Malcolm disliked his work at the mill, which was monotonous, noisy, and ill-paying. He did not stop to consider that he was unqualified for anything else. He lived at home, for he hadn't money to live elsewhere. He was rude to his mother and sister. He had taken up with a bad crowd in town. His particular crony was one Travis Gann, who painted utility poles with creosote at the mill. As a consequence of that pervasive odor, it was impossible for Travis to sneak up on anyone. His whole house smelled of it. Even his dog stank of the tarry substance. Travis, who did not have a mother to keep him in check, had all of Malcolm's bad habits and tendencies, but he had a few more years of experience than Malcolm. Malcolm was, in a sense, apprenticing himself to Travis Gann and his ways.

Queenie knew about Travis Gann. She knew that her son went with Travis to the racetrack in Cantonement on Saturday, and lost what money he had not spent on liquor the night before. She knew that when Malcolm went out of the house after supper he was on his way to Travis's. Malcolm's clothes began to smell of creosote.

One Saturday afternoon, as Queenie and James were driving back from Pensacola and passed a road sign pointing toward Cantonement, Queenie said, "I bet if we went over to the dog track we'd find Malcolm and Travis Gann, betting all their money. James, I wish you would go to Oscar and tell him to fire that man Travis. That would make me very happy."

James protested, "You cain't fire a man because he's taken up with your boy, Queenie. If it wasn't Travis Gann it'd be somebody else. You know that. Malcolm just takes after Carl, I guess."

Queenie shook her head ruefully, and sighed. "What am I gone do?" she said softly.

Queenie was wrong, however. Her son and Travis Gann were not in Cantonement. In Queenie's car they had driven out on the forest road that led eventually to Bay Minette and Mobile. Six miles out of Perdido they pulled up before a weather-beaten, dusty general store. A tin Coca-Cola sign above the door bore one word: Crawford's. Both young men got out, carrying shotguns that had belonged to Carl Strickland.

They went into the store, which was as weather-beaten and dusty within as without. Two long aisles of grimy shelving led back to a grimy counter on which there were large glass jars of cookies and a cash register. Beyond this was a green baize curtain which evidently opened into the house behind the store. Behind the counter stood a weather-beaten and worn-looking middle-aged woman, who said timidly, "You boys ought not bring those guns in here. I'm scared of guns. My daddy shot my mama by mistake when I was a little girl."

Travis Gann said, "You give us all the money you got and we'll take our guns back out."

"You gone shoot me?" she asked.

Travis Gann raised his gun, took aim at her, and grinned. "No, ma'am," he said, but did not lower the weapon.

The woman trembled, and falteringly pressed a key of the cash register. She put all the money from the single small drawer of the register into a penny sack that was intended for the cookies from the glass jars. During this transaction Malcolm stood near the door watching apprehensively for anyone's approach. Travis Gann went closer to the woman and took the money.

"You...gone shoot me?" the lady faltered again.

35

"You got any money in back there?" said Travis Gann, pointing toward the back.

The woman shook her head. "Dial's back there. Dial's my husband. He's not right," she whispered, tapping her temple. "Better stay out of there."

"You got money back there," said Travis Gann, casually lifting the rifle in the crook of one arm so that it was pointed at the woman's stomach.

"Let's go!" cried Malcolm. "Somebody coming down the road."

"Bye-bye," said Travis Gann with a smile and a wink. He and Malcolm ran to the car, awkwardly secreting the shotguns from the sight of those in the oncoming vehicle. As Malcolm started the engine, the car he had seen approaching drove right on past.

"Let's go back," said Travis Gann. "She's got money in the back."

"No," said Malcolm, moving the car swiftly back onto the road. "Lord God, Travis, I was scared to death in there! I thought for sure you were gone blow that old lady's head off!"

"I wisht I had," Travis mused. "I never done that before."

Dollie Faye Crawford ran back into the house and got her husband's gun. She didn't know whether or not it was loaded. She dashed to the front door of the store and peered through the screen. She just got a glimpse of the car as it sped off and in the dust she couldn't read the numbers on the license plate. By the colors, however, she knew that it was an Alabama tag. She went to the telephone and called the Perdido police and said to Charley Key: "This is Dollie Faye Crawford out on the Bay Minette road. Two boys just robbed me. They were driving in a dark blue Ford, about a '34 I'd say, with Alabama tags. They took off in your direction. One of 'em smelled just like creosote."

36

"How much did they take?" the sheriff asked.

"Everything I had," replied Mrs. Crawford.

"Miz Crawford, I'll do what I can. You call up and speak to the Bay Minette police, too, you hear?"

"The creosote man said he was gone shoot me, but he didn't," said Mrs. Crawford, and then she hung up the telephone.

There were only two dark blue '34 Fords in Perdido. One belonged to the high school principal's wife; the other was Queenie Strickland's. Charley Key rode by the high school principal's house, and hollered out the window to the principal, who was watering his grass, "You been out robbing stores this afternoon?"

"No!" shouted the principal. "I haven't got time for foolishness!"

Queenie Strickland's automobile was not in front of her house. Inside, Lucille told the sheriff that Malcolm and Travis Gann had taken the car out about an hour before, but hadn't said where they were going.

"Old Travis," said Sheriff Key, "he works at the mill, don't he?"

"Yes, sir," replied Lucille. "And he just *stinks* of that old creosote. I don't let him come near me! You want to see one of them, Sheriff?"

"I want to see 'em both."

"You want me to give 'em a message?"

"I want to sit on your front porch and wait for 'em to come home is what I want. What's your name?"

"Lucille."

"Lucille," said the sheriff, "you got some iced tea? I sure am hot."

CHAPTER 45

Dollie Faye

Malcolm Strickland and Travis Gann were arrested that evening by Charley Key, charged with armed robbery, and thrown into the five-cell lockup in the Perdido town hall. Queenie and James appeared there about ten minutes after the doors had been slammed shut on the two men.

Malcolm sat sullenly on a bench against the outside wall, shading his eyes from the harsh glare of the single electric bulb dangling from the ceiling. "Don't say it, Ma."

"Say what?" demanded Queenie. "That you're no good? That you've finally done it this time? Well, I will say it. You're no good, Malcolm Strickland. You certainly have done it this time. And you, Travis Gann," she turned to the smirking man sprawled in another corner of the cell, "you put my boy up to this."

"Lord, Miz Strickland," drawled Travis, his creosote stench filling the cell, "I couldn't have talked Malcolm into doing anything he didn't want to do."

"Mama, Uncle James, are you gone get me out, or are you just gone stand there and preach?"

Queenie wouldn't reply.

"We're gone get you out," said James softly.

"Good," said Malcolm. Both men rose.

"Not you, Mr. Gann," said James Caskey.

"Aw, hey..." he protested. "I don't have no rich relatives to pay my bail."

"Then you'll just have to stay in here and rot," said Queenie. "Malcolm, are you gone promise me before you get out of here?"

"Promise you what, Mama?" asked Malcolm apprehensively.

"That you are never gone have anything more to do with this man in your entire life?"

Travis Gann grinned.

"Sure. Mama, you know how much we got?" Malcolm said ruefully, glancing at Travis. "We got twenty-three dollars."

James shook his head. "It's costing me a hundred to get you out of here."

Charley Key appeared with the keys of the cell in his hand.

"Mama," said Malcolm in a low voice, reaching for his mother through the bars, "am I gone go to jail?"

"Where do you belong?" she returned tartly. "You belong in jail for putting James and me through this shame."

"Evening, James," said the sheriff. "Evening, Miz Strickland. You got a lousy excuse for a son here."

"I was just telling him that, Sheriff," said Queenie. "But he's not as bad as his friend there."

"Your mama's got a tongue," remarked Travis Gann, as Malcolm was being let out of the cell. "Miz Strickland, you ought to watch that tongue of yours.

Someday somebody might come up to you and tear it out of your head and wrap it around your neck and choke you to death with it. And who'd get you out of jail *then*, Malcolm?"

"Watch out, Travis," murmured the sheriff. "Don't go threatening people now. Somebody might start to take you serious, and lift your chin with a rifle barrel. Lift it right through the top of your damned head."

Queenie pulled Malcolm a few feet along the corridor out of Travis Gann's sight—but not out of range of his laughter. "Let's go," she said to James.

James was in front of another cell, chatting with two former mill employees; they had been hired by James thirty years before. They were in jail for brawling. "Hey," he was saying, "you two are too old to be fighting over a woman. And you're too poor to be fighting over money. What was it?"

"Plain old hard times," replied the one.

"Nothing else to do," returned the other.

Outside, James paid both men's bail.

Out on the Bay Minette road, in the house in back of Crawford's store, Dollie Faye Crawford had taken to her bed. She was surrounded by neighbors and relatives who had flocked to her in the time of her distress. It was universally judged that she had almost had a stroke. Her blood pressure, as a result of the terrifying incident, was dangerously high. Her husband Dial rocked peaceably in a corner of the room out of everyone's way.

The store was shut, but friends and relatives bearing gifts of food and consolation out of Bibles marked with scraps of paper knocked on the side door of the house. They were admitted by a faded little girl who had been given a pocketful of cookies from one of the jars on the counter of the store in payment for the task. At around eleven o'clock on Sunday morning, the day after the robbery, everyone had gone off to church, and Dollie Faye and Dial were left alone. There was a timid knock at the door, and the little girl opened it.

"Who is it?" called Dollie Faye weakly. "Who's not going to church this morning?"

Into the room walked two visitors the likes of which Dollie Faye and Dial Crawford weren't accustomed to—town people, moneyed people; people whose clothes were new, store-bought, and neither dusty nor faded.

"Yes, ma'am, yes, sir, what can I do for you?" said Dollie Faye, attempting to rise from the bed.

"Don't you dare get out of that bed, Miz Crawford!" cried Queenie.

"Miz Crawford," said James, "you probably don't know us from Adam and his little sister, but Queenie and I have come to apologize and make amends."

"For what?" said Dollie Faye, still trying to get out of bed. Queenie went around and put a stop to *that*.

"It was my boy," said Queenie in a low doleful voice, "who pointed a gun at your head yesterday!"

Dollie Faye fell back against the pillow in surprise.

"Your boy!"

"Yes, ma'am," said James.

"He is no good," said Queenie. "I could *kill* him for scaring you like he did."

"Your boy smell of creosote?"

"No, ma'am," said James. "That was the other boy. That was Travis Gann. He *is* no good."

Dollie Faye, who seemed to have recovered slightly, turned to Queenie and said, "Your boy wasn't the one who said he was gone kill me. It was the other one—the one who smelled like creosote. Your boy didn't want to be there. I could see it in his face. He was 'bout as scared as I was."

42

"*I'd* like to scare him," said Queenie vehemently. She took a chair beside the bed, and leaned forward confidingly. "I'm gone tell you something, Miz Crawford," she said in a low voice. "My boy Malcolm takes after his daddy. His daddy was in the pen, more than once, though I am ashamed to have to say it. The best thing I can say about Malcolm's daddy is that he has been dead for the last five years."

"Now Miz Crawford," James said, glancing at Dial and seeing instinctively that he was not to be an active part of any of this business, "we have brought you some money to make up for what those boys took."

"I nearly forgot, I was so busy apologizing!" cried Queenie, and opened her purse. She handed ten twenty-dollar bills to Dollie Faye.

Dollie Faye cried, "This is so much! I only had twenty dollars in the register yesterday. What'd they do with all them pennies, anyway?"

"Spent 'em at the track," said Queenie with a vigorous nodding of her head. "Every damn one! Oh, 'scuse me, Miz Crawford. I didn't walk in this house with the intention of swearing in your face."

"Y'all call me Dollie Faye."

"Dollie Faye," said James, "Queenie and I want to know what we can do for you."

"Not a thing more, thank you," replied Dollie Faye hastily. "I am taken care of. People have been real good. And you have given me *too much* money."

"When are you gone be able to get out of this bed?" asked Queenie.

"Doctor says I ought to be here a week. See, I've got pressure trouble. Mama died of it. But I'm gone be all right. I *got* to be all right, 'cause I got to get up and run that store. Dial—that's my husband over there in the corner—don't even know how to run the register. And don't know much about stock neither, when it comes down to it. Sometimes I let him wash off windshields, but not much more than that. Used to have a boy to pump gas, but he run off somewheres..."

"You're not gone get out of that bed," said James Caskey sternly.

"I wish I could stay in it," said Dollie Faye, "but there's people 'round here depend on me and this store."

"I'm gone run it," said Queenie, squeezing Dollie Faye's hand.

"You?!"

"I used to work in the Ben Franklin up in Nashville, the big store they had up there. I know how to work a register."

"Queenie's real quick," James assured her.

"But you cain't just up and run my store for me!"

"I know why you're refusing," said Queenie in a low earnest voice. "It's 'cause you don't want the mother of the boy that put a gun to your head hanging around. You don't want to have to look in her suffering face."

"No! It's just that it's so much trouble out here. There's always somebody wanting something special that only I know anything about, and—"

"Cain't I step back in here and ask you things?"

"I guess you could..."

"It's settled then," said Queenie firmly.

"You cain't pump gas," objected Dollie Faye.

"My boy can," whispered Queenie, leaning forward. "See, I'm gone make him quit his job at the mill. He wasn't any good at it anyway, and I don't want him hanging around with those men—he might find himself another Travis Gann. I'm gone bring him out here and make him work off what he stole from you. But you're not even gone see him, I'm not gone let him step foot in this store. Just looking at him might send your pressure up. I saw that little bench out in front, and he's gone sit out there all

44

day long pumping gas, and if Mr. Crawford's weary of washing windshields, then let him take his ease, 'cause Malcolm will do it for him."

On the following day, the Crawfords' store was opened again, and Queenie Strickland had installed herself behind the counter in her second-best dress. Malcolm was out front pumping gas as instructed. James was there too, and he sat and visited with Dollie Faye, every now and then addressing a remark to Dial Crawford, who nodded sagely and kept rocking. At noontime and with Dollie Faye's permission, a very red-faced Malcolm was ushered inside and made a stammering apology. Dollie Faye said, "What you did was wrong, and you near about broke your sweet mama's heart. But I forgive you, Malcolm, for her sake and for your own."

For the next two weeks Queenie presided over the store; Malcolm went on pumping gas, and James continued to sit beside Dollie Faye's bed. Even when Dollie Faye had recovered and resumed her place behind the counter, Queenie and James were not much less assiduous in their attendance on her, and Malcolm kept his place at the pumps. Malcolm's trial was scheduled for the first Wednesday in November, the day after the elections. Queenie drove Dollie Faye to the Bay Minette courthouse and sat with her in the courtroom all the morning long. There were two murders to be tried before the armed robberies came up and the two women observed the proceedings with interest.

Malcolm and Travis were tried together. Dollie Faye testified to the events of that September Saturday. Travis Gann had threatened to blow her head off, he had raised his gun and taken aim, he had carried the money off himself. Obviously ill at ease during the robbery, Malcolm Strickland had cautioned against violence. Dollie Faye was convinced that he had been roped into the whole business completely against his will. She testified that she believed that Malcolm would have come to her rescue had Travis actually attempted to kill her. Moreover, since the crime, Malcolm had more than made up the money that had been taken from her by assisting with the running of the store. Everybody in the courtroom had seen him pumping gas, changing oil, and washing windshields. Dollie Faye had nothing but good to say about Malcolm Strickland and his mother and his uncle, who had been good to her like good Christians ought to be.

After Dollie Faye's testimony Malcolm Strickland was let off with a reprimand, while Travis Gann was sentenced to five years in the Atmore penitentiary.

At the defendants' table, the two young men looked at each other.

"I guess," said Malcolm, "it looks like I'm out and you're in."

"I guess," said Travis Gann with a grin that Malcolm did not expect.

"Hey," said Malcolm, "five years—that's a long time. I'm sorry..."

"Don't be sorry," said Travis, still with the grin. "They're sending me to Atmore. You know how hard it is to get out of Atmore?"

Malcolm shook his head, grateful that because of the court decision he had no use for such information.

"Getting out of Atmore," said Travis, "is like climbing over a rotten log in some old farmer's pasture, that's what getting out of Atmore is like."

"You ought to wait till you get in there, before you start thinking about getting out," warned Malcolm.

"No, not me. I'm already thinking about what I'm gone be doing once I'm free."

The senseless grin seemed to be frozen on Travis's face and it was beginning to make Malcolm uneasy.

Queenie and Dollie Faye were beckoning to him. Malcolm turned back to Travis and asked: "What you gone do, Travis?"

"I'm gone teach some people a lesson, that's what I'm gone do."

"Who you talking about?"

"I'm talking about people walking around free that ought to be in jail with their friends, that's the first kind I'm talking about." Just in case Malcolm had not understood this, Travis Gann punctuated the statement by poking a finger against Malcolm's chest.

"And I'm talking about an old lady who don't mind seeing her boy's best friend get himself in real trouble. An old lady," Travis went on with greater specificity, "who had just as soon see me rot in jail as not." Travis turned his grin toward Queenie and called out, "Hey, Miz Strickland, you better come get your boy here 'fore I get him in any more trouble."

At this, Queenie marched over and took Malcolm's arm. She said, "Travis Gann, you got what you deserved. I'm not a bit sorry for you."

"I know that," Travis said, still grinning. "I know it very well. But maybe someday you will be. Sorry, I mean."

Queenie took Malcolm out of the courtroom. Travis Gann was returned to his cell to await transfer to Atmore. Two more defendants took the young men's place at the table, and Alabama law and justice continued.

That afternoon, sick of pumping gas and even sicker of his enforced penitence, Malcolm Strickland stole his mother's car, drove to Mobile, and joined the army. He did not think it necessary to tell his mother of Travis Gann's thinly veiled threats. It couldn't be *that* easy to escape from Atmore.

CHAPTER 46

Sacred Heart

After Miriam's departure for college, Sister remained aloof from her brother Oscar and his wife. But one evening in November, Sister sat in her dining room alone, eating leftovers and gazing out the window at Oscar's house next door. She could see her brother and his family having supper in their dining room. Frances was talking, and Oscar and Elinor were laughing at whatever it was their daughter was saying. Sister could even faintly hear their voices. She had a sudden revelation. She ran out and across the sandy yard, then called up toward the dining room window, "Hey, Oscar! Elinor!"

Elinor came to the window, and peered out into the evening gloom. "Sister?"

"Can I come in for a few minutes?"

"Of course you can. Come on in." Elinor went into the front hallway.

"Elinor," said Sister as she stepped inside the

house, "I want to apologize. I cain't *imagine* what I was thinking of."

"Thinking of when?"

Oscar appeared in the dining room doorway with his crushed napkin in his hand and his mouth still full of food. "Hey, Sister, how you?"

"Oscar, you know how I am. I'm as lonesome over there as an old rail fence stretching off into nowhere."

"Then why haven't you come to see us before?"

Sister went into the dining room, sat at the table, and accepted the cup of coffee that Zaddie brought to her. "I don't know where my head could have been," said Sister.

"Sister, what *are* you talking about?" said Oscar.

"The reason I haven't come to visit was because of Mama and Miriam. Neither one of 'em ever came here any more than they absolutely had to."

Oscar and Elinor nodded in silent assent.

"But Mama's dead and Miriam's gone off to school, and I was sitting there all alone, seeing your lights over here, thinking, 'Well, I cain't go over there, Mama'd kill me or Miriam wouldn't speak to me.' Then all of a sudden I realized how foolish I was being, so here I am."

Oscar laughed. "Sister, those two had you *trained*."

"They sure did!"

"I hope you're going to come over and see us all the time, now," said Elinor.

"I sure would like to," sighed Sister. "And maybe I will."

"What's going to stop you?" asked Elinor.

"Who knows?" said Sister darkly. "That's the problem with this family—you cain't count on anything staying the same for long."

Thereafter, Elinor and Oscar wouldn't hear of Sister's eating supper by herself in that dark old house. In the afternoon, Elinor frequently called across the yard, "Sister, come on over here and keep me company." Sometimes, Sister and Elinor went shopping together. "Elinor," Sister once said, "you married Oscar seventeen years ago. We've all grown old since then, but this is the first time you and I have spent any time together. I get mad at Mama and Miriam when I think of all the things they kept me from doing."

"Blame Mary-Love," returned Elinor. "Don't blame Miriam. Miriam wasn't grown up. You could have told Miriam what to do, and Miriam would have had to do it. You were weak, Sister. But after being brought up by that mama of yours, I don't see how you could have been any other way."

There were other alterations in the relationships within the Caskey family that autumn. When Malcolm ran away to join the army, Queenie was distraught, and begged James to send somebody to fetch him back. But James argued that Malcolm was twenty-one and could do what he pleased. "Besides," James pointed out while they were choosing an automobile to replace the one that Malcolm had stolen, "you have always said that what Malcolm needed was a good dose of army discipline." So Queenie allowed herself to be lightened of the burden that had been her son. She no longer worried about him, but indulged herself to a greater extent than ever before in James's company. Lucille complained that her mother was never at home, and that she always knew where to find her, which was over at Uncle James's. James and Queenie gossiped, James and Queenie went shopping in Pensacola and Mobile, James and Queenie had no secrets from one another. Then they began making visits in Perdido as a couple. Some lady in town would say to her friend, "I'm bored to death. Let's call up James and Queenie and see if they won't come over and talk a spell." Or another lady would say, "Let's ride by James's house and see if Queenie and him are out on the porch."

Together, Queenie and James paid visits to Elinor. Often they found Sister with her. These visits soon lost the formal aspect that they had had at first; they became as easy and natural as Perdido had always thought they should be, with all the Caskeys living in adjacent houses. Soon the households began taking meals together. It seemed foolish to have Zaddie, Roxie, and Ivey cooking three complete different meals when everyone might meet at Elinor's for the big meal of the day and enjoy themselves more. The three black women got together early in the morning, planned the meal, then retired to their separate kitchens to prepare their individual parts. In midmorning, Roxie and Ivey could be seen bearing steaming pots and casseroles across the sandy yards beneath the water oaks. Everyone gathered at noon. James or Oscar said grace, and for an hour the Caskeys were as happy as any family had the right to be.

One day Oscar, from his usual spot at the head of the table, said, "Y'all, I just thought of something. None of this would have been possible when Mama was alive. She would never have let us do this."

Everyone at the table grew quiet. Everyone knew that Oscar spoke the truth, and the indictment against Mary-Love was telling.

Ivey, bringing in a plate of hot rolls, said, "Miss Mary-Love didn't like to see nobody rich, 'less she was the one put the fi' dollar in their hand."

Roxie, who was serving iced tea, said, "Miss Mary-Love didn't like to see nobody happy 'less she was the one put happiness in their head."

Zaddie, holding open the kitchen door, said, "Miss Mary-Love wouldn't speak to me, just 'cause I belonged to Miss El'nor and not to her. If Miss Mary-

Love was to see all of you here together, she'd fall down to the floor in a fit!"

There was another moment of silence, as Mary-Love Caskey was remembered by her family.

"Mama's dead, though," said Sister, lifting her glass with a slight smile.

After this noontime meal, when Oscar had returned to the mill, Lucille to the Ben Franklin store, and Danjo and Frances to the high school, the others usually went upstairs and sat on the screened porch with more glasses of iced tea. One afternoon a few days before Thanksgiving, Queenie, Sister, Elinor, and James were on the porch making plans for the holiday meal, when Luvadia Sapp made an appearance in the doorway and said, "Mr. James, they's a car out in front of your house, and somebody getting out."

"Who is it?"

"Don't know."

Everybody rose and peered out. They could see only a corner of the automobile parked in front of James's house.

"I better go down and see," said James.

Everybody went down to see, and what everybody saw was James's daughter Grace, striding up the sidewalk with two enormous suitcases.

After graduation from Vanderbilt, Grace had taught physical education at a girls' school in Spartanburg, South Carolina, and had lived with another young woman whom the Caskeys always referred to as "Grace's particular friend." At first this particular friend's name was Georgia, but then it altered itself to Louise, and later to Catherine. So far as Grace's father and the rest of the family knew, Grace was perfectly happy, and that, despite the unorthodox manner of her achieving such contentment, was all that really mattered.

"Grace!" called James.

"Daddy!"

Grace, twenty-six now, appeared stronger and sturdier than ever. The suitcases appeared to weigh nothing as she swung them onto the porch. Everyone gathered around her, and James cried, "Darling, I didn't know you were coming back for Thanksgiving."

"I am home for good and all," said Grace defiantly.

"No!" cried everyone. And: "Grace, what happened?!"

"Grace," said her father, "is something wrong? What about your friend Catherine?"

"Oh, Catherine left that school year before last, Daddy! I told you that." She sighed. "It was Mildred this time."

"Did you two girls have an argument?" asked Queenie solicitously.

"I hate her!" cried Grace. "And I don't want to talk about Mildred, 'cause I'm never gone see her again. If she calls and wants to speak to me, tell her I've moved to Baton Rouge or somewhere. Have y'all eaten? I am famished. I have driven straight through from Atlanta."

"What did Mildred do to make you so unhappy?" asked her father. "I thought you liked that school."

Grace pursed her lips. "*She's gone get married.* And, Daddy, I don't want to hear another word about Mildred, 'cause it just drives me crazy even to think about her. Y'all," she said to her family in general, "I loved that girl to the bottom of my soul, and now she up and tells me she is gone go off and marry some old man that sells property in Miami! So nobody ever mention her name to me again!"

"You've quit your job?" asked Elinor.

"I have. Daddy, you're gone have to support me. I am weary unto death of giving away my heart to people that don't deserve it."

"Good for you, Grace," said Queenie. "We are so glad to have you back—you cain't imagine how we have missed you. I never laid eyes on Mildred in my life, but one thing I know for sure is, she didn't deserve *you*."

No more was learned about why Grace gave up her employment at the Spartanburg girls' school, but somehow the rumor in Perdido arose that Grace had not abandoned her position voluntarily, that she had been ousted from it in some obscure but serious disgrace. Grace Caskey, though, never acted as if she had returned to Perdido in dishonor. She tackled this new stage of her life with energy and resolve. The day after her unexpected reappearance she went to the principal of the high school, showed him her certificates, and said, "Let me coach the girls' basketball team."

"We don't have one," the principal replied.

"Then I'll form one," said Grace. "And in the spring we'll talk about softball."

She formed a girls' basketball team, drilled her girls relentlessly, and then drove them all over five counties of Alabama and Florida to play other teams. She taught dancing classes at Lake Pinchona that winter, and itched for warm weather so that she could start lessons in diving and water-rescue. She put on her high boots to go rattlesnake hunting with the boys in the high school. She put on a straw hat and stood with Roxie on the Baptist Bottom bridge, fishing for bream in the lower Perdido.

"I remember," said James to Queenie, "when Grace was little, I couldn't hardly get her to sit on the back steps on a sunshiny day. She was so shy she'd run and hide anytime somebody knocked on the front door. Now I cain't even *begin* to keep up with her, and if I want her to stay in the house for five minutes, I have to rope her to the breakfront."

Grace's phenomenal energy was exceeded only by

her appetite. She was in the kitchen half an hour before dinner every afternoon, fishing out pieces of chicken and getting her hand slapped by Roxie, who still thought of her as a little girl. At table, she always called for more chopped steak, more little green peas, more creamed corn, more rolls, more butter, and greedily snatched whatever was left on the serving plates when everybody else was filled to bursting. She was the first to sit down and the last to get up. She never appeared to gain weight.

At table one afternoon in mid-December of 1938, Grace at last pushed her plate away, signaled for one final glass of tea, and said, "Well, somebody tell me how Miriam's doing down at Sacred Heart."

All the Caskeys looked at one another.

"Nobody knows," answered Elinor at last.

"What do you mean?" demanded Grace. "Hasn't anybody written to her?"

"She doesn't answer," said Sister, appearing suddenly troubled.

Grace looked around astounded. "You mean that poor child went away in September, and nobody's spoken to her since?"

"How?" asked Oscar with a shrug of helplessness. "Miriam does what she wants. If Miriam wanted to speak to us, we figure she'd write or call. She didn't tell anybody where she was going until the very morning she left. Nobody wanted to interfere, Grace. But I guess," he said, looking around the table, "that maybe we've let it go a little too long..."

The fact was that Miriam reminded them all too much of Mary-Love. While none of them ever actually had said it aloud, the Caskeys, reunited after so many years of division and animosity, had not felt any great desire to have Miriam return to provoke old hostilities. Even Sister, who loved her most, had been glad that she had stayed away. However, not one of them, even for a single moment of the three

56

months of her absence, ever worried that Miriam might not be well, or content with the lot she had chosen for herself.

"Well," said Grace, with her hands on her hips, "I have never seen or heard of the like. I want y'all to look at me." Everybody did as they were told. "When I get up from this table, I am going to drive directly down to Mobile and the Sacred Heart College and see Miriam, and I am going to ask her to her own face how she is getting along. Has anybody even *thought* to ask her if she's coming home for Christmas?"

No one had.

"Maybe...I should go with you," said Sister tentatively.

"Maybe you should," said Grace firmly. She rose from the table.

In five minutes, Grace and Sister were on their way to Mobile to see Miriam.

Sacred Heart College was a school run by Jesuits, located on the far western side of Mobile on about fifty acres of lawn, oak, azaleas, and cypress. Its buildings were of stodgy, scrubbed brick. The students themselves were stodgy and scrubbed—girls intensely devoted to the Roman Catholic religion, to their Jesuit teachers, and to one another. They lived three to a room in grim brick dormitories, whose chaste gray interiors were in dispiriting contrast to the intense and manicured vegetation that covered the college's campus.

Grace easily found the Administration Building and, from a nun in the registrar's office, got the location of Miriam's room. Grace and Sister were gently chided for the unannounced midweek visit, which wasn't at all customary, and which would doubtless have a disruptive effect.

"We couldn't help it," said Grace, uncowed. "You

see, Miriam's daddy's sister died last night, and we have come to tell Miriam the bad news."

Alarmed and moved, the nun summoned a gardener to show Grace and Sister across the campus to Miriam's dormitory.

At the dormitory, the doleful news had already been received by the house mistress, and Grace and Sister were shown up to Miriam's room directly.

"I cain't believe," whispered Sister fretfully, "that we have just gone and lied to a bunch of *nuns*. Telling them that I am dead!"

"Hush," hissed Grace.

The house mistress knocked on Miriam's door, and then respectfully retreated.

Grace didn't wait for the knock to be answered. She opened the door, without being bidden.

In the small gray room were three narrow beds, each covered with a gray blanket; three tiny desks were topped with small green blotters; three chests-of-drawers were stacked one atop the other; and there was a standing wardrobe with double doors. On one of the beds, beneath a window, lay Miriam, weeping convulsively against her pillow. The nun, Grace thought, must already have told her the bad news.

She looked up incredulously and gaped at Sister and Grace in the doorway.

"You poor darling!" cried Grace, holding open her arms wide.

Miriam sat tentatively up on the bed, and then after only a moment's hesitation, rushed across the room and took refuge in Grace's embrace.

"Honey," cried Sister, "I'm not dead! Grace, you shouldn't have told the nun that lie!"

"What?" stammered Miriam.

"Come hug me!" cried Sister, and took Miriam away from Grace. "They came and told you I was dead, didn't they? That's why you were crying, wasn't it?"

"No," said Miriam, mystified and still sniffling.

"Then why were you crying?" said Sister.

Miriam drew back, and looked at Grace. "Because I'm always crying," returned Miriam.

"What!" said Sister. "You never cried before in your life, Miriam! Not even when you were little and Ivey Sapp dropped you on the crown of your head!"

Miriam pulled away and retreated once more to her bed. She dried her eyes on her handkerchief. "Why are you here?" she asked.

"We came to see if you were all right," said Grace, hopping up onto one of the desks and crossing her legs beneath her. "But I can see that you're not, are you?"

"I hate it here!"

"Why!" cried Sister. "Miriam, we didn't have any idea! Why didn't you just call me and tell me you were unhappy?"

" 'Cause you were so glad to get rid of me, that's why!"

"No, I wasn't! I didn't want you to leave me! I wanted to keep you with me forever and ever."

"Nobody else wanted me there in Perdido," said Miriam.

"Everybody misses you a lot," said Sister reassuringly. "Frances talks about you all the time. She is pining away."

"You were homesick, weren't you?" said Grace.

Miriam glanced at Grace sharply, then nodded her head. "Yes, very homesick."

"Then why in the world," said Sister, "didn't you come home?"

"Nobody asked me."

"Nobody had to *ask* you," cried Sister in exasperation. "Darling, that house is yours, and we're all your family. You could have come home every weekend, and we would always have been glad to see you. Ivey's dying to cook for you again. Your room is always kept ready. In fact, nobody knows what to do without you."

"I hate this old place," repeated Miriam, glancing distastefully about her room.

"You don't like your roommates?" said Grace.

"I hate them, and they hate me."

"I bet they're real sweet," said Sister vaguely. "Hey, Miriam, why didn't you come home for Thanksgiving? We had an empty chair."

"Nobody asked me."

"Lord God!" cried Sister. "What were we supposed to do, send a herald and an engraved invitation? Miriam, we are your *family*. Don't you know it?"

At last Miriam's eyes were dry. Now she was sullen.

After a few moments of glancing first at Miriam and then at Sister, Grace said energetically, "Miriam, when does your Christmas vacation begin?"

"Friday."

"All right then, Sister and I will be back then to get you. You are coming back to Perdido for the holidays—and not another word on the subject. If you have made other plans, then you break 'em, 'cause you're not getting out of this."

"A girl in my history class *had* asked me to go home with her to New Orleans," said Miriam hesitantly.

"Don't you do it," said Grace sternly. "You're coming home with us. Sister and I will be here on Friday."

"I don't need you," said Miriam. "I've got my car. I'll be in Perdido by suppertime."

"Sister and I will come down anyway," said Grace. "We've got some Christmas shopping to do down here, and we'll drop by here to help you pack up."

To be thus taken in hand and ordered to come to Perdido seemed exactly what Miriam wanted. She ventured a smile, and said she was glad that Grace and Sister had come to see her. She offered to show them around the campus, and after that brief tour she introduced her relatives to her roommates. There was some awkwardness in maintaining the deception of a dead relative in the light of Miriam's obviously improved temper. When questioned about this by one of the nuns, Grace explained boldly, "False alarm. It was just a stroke, and we hear that she's much better now."

That evening, Grace and Miriam and Sister went out to dinner together at the Government House in downtown Mobile, and there Miriam shamefacedly admitted the harrowing extent of her homesickness. "I cried every night before I went to bed, and I cried every morning when I got up. I never thought I could miss old Perdido so much, and everybody there. I used to daydream about walking along the levee, and buying bobby pins down at the Ben Franklin."

"Honey, I wish you'd called or written and told us how miserable you were," said Sister plaintively.

"She's just like Mary-Love," said Grace abruptly. "And it's always somebody else who has to make the first step. Miriam, you know that's how you are, and Mary-Love taught you some bad lessons. It's about time you got over a little of that."

Sister was certain that this straightforward talk would inflame Miriam, who was very touchy on the subject of her dead grandmother, but Miriam, apparently chastened by her unhappiness, only replied, "I sure will be glad to sleep in my own bed. I am sick to death of having to share everything. And after New Year's, I know I'm gone dread leaving Perdido again."

CHAPTER 47

The Causeway

Miriam had learned a hard lesson during her three-month sojourn at Sacred Heart College. She had discovered that she was not as strong and independent as she had thought. From the first night she had been assailed by loneliness, homesickness, insecurity, and unhappiness. She had liked nothing about Sacred Heart: its buildings, its grounds, its teachers, its students. All were strange to her. The nuns were threatening. The girls in the dormitory all seemed privy to a secret about life that Miriam could not figure out. Despite what she told her family, she had decided against converting to Catholicism. The more she saw of that religion, the less it agreed with her. Though she never would have admitted it, even to herself, Miriam wasn't entirely sure why she had chosen Sacred Heart over any other school. Perhaps because it was so close to Perdido—even though she had left home with the intention of returning only infrequently. Perhaps because only women went there—to prevent the family from having any satisfaction in imagining that she even remotely contemplated marriage. Perhaps only because, of all colleges, Sacred Heart had seemed unlikeliest for her.

Even in her first days there, she missed Perdido. Often she thought of the house in which she had grown up. She thought about her room and Mary-Love's room and Sister's room. She thought of Ivey in the kitchen, and longed to hear Luvadia's rake scratching patterns in the sandy yard. She wanted to hear the creak of the rotting water oak limbs outside her window. She thought of the Perdido, flowing always swiftly, always turbulently behind its protective wall of red clay. She wanted, from the moment she set foot on the Sacred Heart campus, to be back in Perdido, to live as she had always lived. She was desperate for Sister's company, and she missed Oscar and Elinor and Frances on one side of the house, and James and Danjo on the other. Once, Miriam went downtown to one of the banks in Mobile, and opened her safety-deposit box and examined the diamonds and sapphires that were hidden within it, but the jewels proved of no comfort. She shut the box and returned to the dormitory to cry.

Miriam never even considered returning to Perdido for the weekend, even though Perdido was less than fifty miles away, no more than an hour and a half's drive in the roadster. Though she missed them woefully, and realized for the first time how much she loved them, Miriam still thought of her family as the enemy. This was her grandmother's teaching, and a lesson by which only Miriam suffered. She waited for some sign of capitulation: a telephone call from Sister to say she was desperately missed, a postcard from Frances to ask when she was coming home, a frantic telegram to demand her presence at Thanksgiving dinner, an ostensibly casual visit from

James and Queenie at the tag end of one of their Mobile shopping excursions. Hearing nothing, she concluded that her family had won, and that she had lost. Grace's visit seemed heaven-sent and Miriam prayed thanks to the God of her classmates.

In the last few days before Christmas vacation began, however, Miriam grew anxious. She perceived that she would be returning in a state of disgrace—and vulnerability. Grace would have told everyone that she had nearly collapsed beneath the weight of homesickness, that she had been desperate for news of home, that she had missed everyone—even her mother and father. Miriam declined Sister and Grace's offer to return to the college and assist her in packing. With great misgiving she drove back to Perdido through the gathering dusk.

She pulled up before the house, got out, carried her bag inside, and called Sister's name. No one was home.

At Sacred Heart, Miriam had suffered a nightmare. In her dream, she had given up her pride and returned to Perdido, only to find that her family had abandoned the three houses along the river and departed without leaving word of their whereabouts. In the gloom of twilight in the empty house the nightmare seemed to have become reality and Miriam trembled. She ran outside, out the back door, and stood dwarfed and trembling beneath the towering water oaks.

"Miriam!" Sister's voice came from above. Miriam looked up. Sister stood at the screens of Oscar and Elinor's upstairs porch. "Everybody's over here, darling!"

Thinking, *They've won, they've won,* Miriam entered her parents' house. Zaddie appeared as a dark shadow in the even darker hallway, and said, "Hey, Miss Miriam, how you?"

"Fine, Zaddie. Just fine," she replied, and slowly climbed the stairs to the second floor.

Everyone was there on the screened porch: her parents, Sister, Frances, Danjo and James and Grace, Queenie and Lucille.

"Hey, y'all," said Miriam softly. "I'm back."

No one crowed triumph.

Her mother said quietly, "Miriam, Grace said you had an invitation to go off with one of your friends, but we are truly pleased that you decided to spend Christmas with us..."

"We are all having supper together over here...in your honor," said Oscar tentatively, " 'cause we are all so glad to see you again, darling."

No more was said about her return. No one pressed its ignominy back upon her; no one trod upon her prostrate spirit.

Miriam sat down in the swing beside Frances, who in a quick, apprehensive motion leaned over and hugged her. Miriam tried to gather her thoughts and think this thing out. She looked over at Grace.

Grace said, "Miriam, when I told everybody that you had decided to come back here for Christmas they were so excited, I cain't tell you!"

That was it then; Grace and Sister had said nothing of her homesickness nor her dire unhappiness at Sacred Heart. She had been defeated by her own emotions and weakness, but no one except Grace and Sister knew it.

Queenie asked her how she liked Sacred Heart.

"It takes some...getting used to," replied Miriam carefully. "I never knew there were so many Catholics before. Some of the mill workers are Catholic— aren't they, Oscar?—but I wasn't used to *everybody* praying to the Virgin, and people telling rosary beads and tacking up little cards with pictures of the crucifixion on them. All of that makes me a little nervous. I'm still not used to it."

Miriam soon discovered that in her absence considerable changes had been wrought in the family. She found that she was expected to go to her parents' house every day for the midday meal, and that her former recalcitrance in the matter wasn't to be indulged. She bridled the first few days to think that she was to converse with her father and mother, with whom she had had almost nothing to do all of her life. But then she realized that they were treating *her* differently.

For the first time, suddenly and radically, Miriam was being regarded as an adult. She had an equal place with Sister, and a greater place, it seemed, than either Frances or Lucille.

Miriam wasn't certain how this promotion had come about.

What Miriam didn't suspect—and never found out—was that Grace and Sister *had* told the Caskeys everything. Everyone knew that Miriam had suffered badly with homesickness, had cried herself to sleep every night, had felt hatred for Sacred Heart and disgust with everything that was not of Perdido. The Caskeys were touched by the revelation. No one had suspected Miriam had such sensitivity; and when she returned for the Christmas holidays, no one threw it in her face.

By New Year's Miriam knew that in a week she must either return to Sacred Heart or declare her intention never to leave Perdido. So far as she knew, no one in her family knew her detestation of the place and her love for her home. She could not now suddenly say, I was miserable at Sacred Heart, and I don't want to go back. Her family wouldn't know what to think, but leaving Perdido again—when Perdido was sweeter than ever to her—seemed an equally impossible course.

Her father solved her problem. On New Year's

Day, as the plates of turkey and pheasant and ham were being passed around the dinner table, Oscar said to his daughter, "Miriam, I wish to God you wouldn't leave us. I have never seen so much of you as in the past few weeks, and it's gone break my heart to see you go back to that college."

"I got to go, Oscar," replied Miriam weakly.

"Not if you don't want to," said Sister. "It's important these days for a girl to have a college education, nobody knows that better than I do, but I wish for once you'd give up your selfish ways and think of me, Miriam. I'm so lonely without you." Sister could now confidently speak of loneliness without anyone pointing out that she might, as a solution, return to her husband in Nashville.

Miriam didn't know what to say. Now that the way had been paved for her staying—now that her family had, in its way, capitulated and begged the mercy of her continued presence in' their midst—it began to seem to Miriam that her months at Sacred Heart hadn't been *so* bad. She had been unhappy, she had cried herself to sleep and awoke each morning with dried tears welding shut her eyes; yet her grades hadn't suffered, and she had liked being so near to the amenities of Mobile. Only with her family asking her to remain in Perdido did returning to Sacred Heart become a possibility.

"Miriam, you remember how last summer we drove to Pensacola every morning?" said Frances tentatively.

"I remember," said Miriam absently.

"Well," Frances went on, "Mobile's not any farther away. Why don't you just drive down there every day? It only takes about an hour."

"It takes longer," said Miriam, looking up with interest now. " 'Cause Sacred Heart's on the far side of town."

"You could still do it," said Sister excitedly. "You

could live at home, drive down to Mobile every morning, and be back in time for supper. I could get Ivey to stay on later, and make you something hot."

"I could do that," said Ivey, coming in from the kitchen at that moment with a dish of creamed corn. "I'd be happy to cook for you, Miss Miriam."

Oscar said, "It's settled then. You're not gone leave us. You're gone drive down to school in the morning and come back in the evening. You will sleep in your own bed and you will keep us all happy."

"This is gone be a whole lot of trouble for me," said Miriam.

"We don't care one bit," said Sister. "You are gone let us impose on you, and we don't care *how* much trouble you're gone have to go through."

The administration of the college said no to Miriam's request to live at home. Miriam, desolate, went to her room and wept. She tearfully telephoned Sister to say that all was off.

Grace appeared at the college at eight o'clock the following morning and spoke to the provost. She told him that Miriam was needed at home in the evening to care for her aunt and guardian who was ill—still recovering from her stroke—and would have no one but Miriam about her. Otherwise, for the sake of the aunt, Miriam would have to be withdrawn from the school. The provost gave in. Miriam packed her bags, shook hands with her roommates, and raced back to Perdido.

Every morning Miriam drove her roadster down to Mobile, attended her classes, and returned home by four or five o'clock in the afternoon. Some days she was home in time for midday dinner. She never complained of the trip, though everyone thought she probably would soon get bored with it. Sometimes Grace or Sister or even her mother rode with her, and spent the day shopping in Mobile. Miriam, though still often abrasive and short, became accustomed to being with her family, and could manage now to sit through a whole meal without growing huffy or taking offense at someone's innocent remark. Her dead grandmother's influence was waning.

She saw no reason to alter her situation during her sophomore year at the college. One day she suggested to her sister Frances, then a senior in the Perdido high school, that she go to Sacred Heart as well. "As long as I'm driving down there every day, you might as well come too."

Frances was delighted with the offer. She had thought of the plan herself, but had not dared put the question to Miriam for fear of an abrupt refusal. Elinor and Oscar were pleased. They still thought of their daughter as frail and dependent. It would be a comfort to them to know that in her first difficult years at college Frances would have Miriam so near. Oscar was a little uneasy that Frances might not withstand conversion to Catholicism as Miriam had, but Elinor assured him that Frances would hold on staunchly to her Methodist principles. Frances applied to Sacred Heart and was accepted. In the autumn of 1940, the roadster's passenger seat was occupied each day by Frances.

It was odd to Frances that, while it was always over the same route, their journey to Mobile in the mornings should be so different from the late afternoon trip home. Leaving Perdido, the road first wound through pine forest—much of it owned by the Caskeys themselves—and then into Bay Minette, the county seat of Baldwin County. The highway led on down to Pine Haven and Stapleton, bleak hamlets occupied mainly by pecan and potato farmers, and then across to Bridgehead. Then there was a wondrously long, straight causeway on either side of which lay marshes, rivers, and islands, all fading imperceptibly one into the other in the early morning light. Rivers were a mile wide here, their sources no more than ten miles upstream. There were vast islands of grass scarcely two feet above the level of the water, where fishermen often disappeared. On both sides of the blacktopped road were vistas of nothing but pink sky, blue water, and green marsh grass. The Blakeley River faded into Dacke Bay which in turn became the Apalachee River. The boundaries were nebulous between all these bodies of water— Chacaloochee Bay, the Tensaw River, Delvan Bay, and the Mobile River.

On those rides to Mobile, begun before either of the sisters was well awake, Frances stared at the water and the sky and the grass, and was reminded not only of the summer she and Miriam had spent on the beach at Pensacola, but of earlier times, hazy times in her past and in her childhood, and of times that, impossibly, lay even further back, before there *was* a Frances Caskey. The top of the car was always down, and the loud wind prevented conversation. The smell of the salt marsh, where all these rivers, estuaries, and streams emptied into the great maw of Mobile Bay, filled Frances's brain. Without actually sleeping, she seemed to dream. The pink sky was bright and empty. The water below was blue and torpid. The wind became a song, without notes or melody or words, but with pitches and rhythms that were wholly familiar to her.

In her dreams, Frances saw the secret things that swam out of sight below the surface of the bright water and stared greedily up at the automobile passing along the causeway. Frances dreamed of what hid in the low grass of the insubstantial marshy islands, and what dead things lay twisted and broken in the ancient mud. She dreamed of what bones were buried in hummocks, saw what tore fishermen's nets, and understood why fishermen themselves sometimes disappeared.

She woke—or ceased to dream—when the roadster emerged from the tunnel that ran beneath the last tendril of the segmented Mobile River. She turned and smiled, and always said, "Oh, we're here already..."

The return trip to Perdido late in the day was different. Clouds defiled the purity of the sky, already darkening in the east ahead of them. The marshes, bays, rivers, and hummocks of grass seemed dirty and sodden. The small towns of Baldwin County were crowded, noisy, and crass. Even the pine forest was dusty and wearying. On the trip home Frances never dreamed, and never remembered what she had dreamed in the morning.

In the evenings she always felt that something was missing, and she longed for the hours to pass, and for dawn to come again. Then in the morning, as Miriam drove over the causeway, Frances would again dream of what lay beneath the surface of the blue trembling water.

CHAPTER 48

Mobilization

Perdido gave scant thought to the war in Europe; the town was for the Allies, against the Axis, and that was that. Perdido was preoccupied with the upward struggle from the severe and repeated assaults of the Depression. Then, like the stunning surprise of a blow to the back of the head, the National Guard was mobilized in November of 1940. One hundred and seventeen young Perdido men were notified that they might be instantly called away. One of the old dormitories below Baptist Bottom that had been used to house levee workers was quickly converted into an armory, and those one hundred and seventeen mill workers, layabouts, and high school seniors congregated there every morning in expectation of marching orders. Christmas and New Year's passed, but no orders came.

Oscar was grateful that no call for the men had yet come; he needed his workers. During the Depression he had provided employment in Perdido that was far beyond the actual manpower needs of the Caskey mills and factories. In recent months, however, activity had picked up sharply. The War Department had placed orders for vast quantities of lumber and posts. Oscar learned that the new Camp Rucca was being built in the Alabama Wiregrass. He heard that Eglin Field, the air base over the Florida line, was tripling its size. Oscar placed notices in the Perdido *Standard* and in the newspapers of Atmore, Brewton, Bay Minette, Jay, Pensacola, and Mobile offering work to those men not yet put on active alert. Some came, but not as many as he had hoped. Many Baldwin and Escambia county boys had already been sent away. Every morning, as he was shaved in the barber's chair, Oscar considered what he could do: hire high school boys in the afternoon, employ women in the lighter jobs that before had been held by men, and promote colored men into jobs that were presently denied them. These strategies were not yet necessary, and only Oscar anticipated a time when they *would* be required.

Oscar had lost some of his buoyancy. The death of Mary-Love and the retirement of James had placed the management of the mill squarely and exclusively upon his shoulders. He had at once to deal with an expanded operation and declining receipts. He was no longer youthful, for that matter, nearly forty-five now, with two daughters in college, and the responsibility for an industry on which the well-being of the entire town was dependent. He had settled into a narrow, strictured life, hemmed in by his family and by the mill. He loved his family, and he was proud of the mill, but sometimes he looked about and wondered. Sometimes his eyes fell upon his wife, and he thought, *Who is she?*

Elinor had changed, most noticeably since the death of Mary-Love. She was a good deal calmer now, less prone to fits of anger; she seemed less dangerous. She hadn't the destructive instincts he had seen in her before. There had been times, Oscar knew, when his wife had been motivated by a kind of unselfish greed—that is, greed for his and Frances's sake, more than for her own. The wellsprings of that loving avarice seemed to have lost some of their strength recently. Oscar occasionally thought of the future of the mill as he and Elinor lay in bed at night, and he would ask Elinor's opinion. He wanted to know what she would do in his place; he wanted to hear what people in town thought about this and that. But Elinor's interest in such conversations had waned. In fact, her interest in nearly everything had diminished to such an extent that Oscar became alarmed, and he suggested that she visit Leo Benquith and get a prescription. He was certain that something was the matter with her.

"Elinor," he asked one night, turning toward her in the darkness. "Tell me something. How old are you?"

"You have never asked me that question before," returned Elinor. "Why are you asking me now?"

Oscar hesitated. "You've been acting so funny, I thought you were pregnant."

Elinor laughed, but her laugh was small and weak.

"I've been thinking," said Elinor.

It suddenly occurred to Oscar that his wife had only been waiting for such a question from him to enable her to speak about something that had oppressed her spirit for some time.

"Thinking about what?" her husband asked gently.

"I was thinking about Miriam and how homesick she got when she first went away to school."

"She sure did. And she didn't let on, either."

"I'm homesick, too, Oscar," said Elinor in a small voice, and wound her arms around her husband's neck in a kind of cold desperation.

"Elinor," he cried in surprise, "I don't believe you have mentioned Wade once in fifteen years."

Elinor paused. "I've thought about it a lot, though."

"Do you have any people who are still alive? I know you never hear from them."

"There's not many of us left, that's true. And we never were big on letters or the telephone."

"Then why don't you just drive on up there and visit with them a spell?"

"I think I might do just that," said Elinor.

"It might do you some good to get away from here. I think you've been cooped up. Perdido's so small. And it's been so long since you were home…"

"It has been," sighed Elinor. "I miss it too. I've been feeling tired lately, peaked, and maybe all I need to get my strength back up is to go home for a little while."

"I wish I could go with you—"

"You can't, Oscar, you're too busy with the mill," said Elinor hastily.

"I know, so take somebody else. Take Sister or Grace or James. I know we'd all like to meet your family. You never talk about them, so I just always forget that you have a family. Somehow I had it in my head that they were all dead."

"As I said, there are some left," said Elinor. "But I think I want to go up there alone."

"You want to get away from us all, don't you? I don't blame you one little bit for that. We're all pretty wearing, aren't we?"

Elinor laughed, and hugged her husband close. There wasn't as much desperation in her embrace now, but her arms around him still felt damp and cold.

Next morning at the barbershop, Oscar thought not about the mill but about his wife. He was pleased to think he had pressed the trigger of her secret—

76

her homesickness for Wade in Fayette County. Of all things that might have depressed or saddened Elinor, absence from her family and early home was the last he would ever have considered. He would see that she got away soon, because he wanted no delay in the recovery of her spirits and energy. When he went home for dinner at noon, he thought, he would encourage her to leave that very week; there was nothing keeping her in Perdido.

When he reached home at noon, he was startled to discover that, without a word, Elinor had already left. Zaddie said, "She got out a suitcase, that small one. She sent Bray off to fill up the car with gas. She told me what all to do while she was gone. And then she took off. I said, 'Miss El'nor, don't you want some chicken?' and she said, 'Zaddie, I'm just *dying* to get home.' She wasn't gone wait for nothing, Mr. Oscar."

"I cain't believe it," said Oscar in amazement. "She didn't even say goodbye."

Zaddie repeated her story for the other members of the family as each arrived for the noontime meal. The Caskeys were perplexed, and every few moments Zaddie was called into the dining room to answer another puzzling question.

"Zaddie, did she call up to Wade first to see if anyone was gone be home?" asked Queenie.

"Did she leave a number where we can get in touch with her?" asked Grace.

"Or an address, so we could send a telegram?" queried James.

"Or did she even say what the people's names were?" wondered Oscar. "I guess maybe they're Dammerts, but I don't think I ever even heard Elinor say for sure. They could be her mama's people, and we never would know how to get in touch with them." He looked around the table. "Has anybody ever been to Wade?"

The Caskeys all shook their heads.

"I never even heard of the place till Elinor said she came from there," said James. "And I had forgot all about it till just now. Who would have thought that Elinor still had any family to go and visit? I don't believe she has mentioned them even once in the past twenty years."

"All I can say," said Sister, "is that she must have been awfully anxious to get up there if she left without saying goodbye to anybody but Zaddie. Oscar, you sure she didn't stop by the mill on her way out of town?"

"I'm sure she didn't," said Oscar.

"She went in the other direction," said Zaddie from the kitchen. "Out toward the Old Federal Road."

Everyone was astounded. "That won't take her anywhere!" cried James. "I hope she had a map with her, 'cause that Old Federal Road just fades out..."

No one could make anything of it. They had no way of getting in touch with Elinor should an emergency arise, and they had no idea of when she intended to return. She had given no indication of the length of her stay. Every day the Caskeys hoped for her reappearance, and nightly Oscar went to bed alone and disappointed. After a week, Grace volunteered to drive up to Wade—wherever in the world it was—and find Elinor, but Oscar said, "No, I don't want you to do that. Elinor's all right, I'm not worried about her. She wanted to get away from us for a bit. After twenty years, I don't hold that against her. We're not gone go traipsing up there and drag her back like we cain't do without her."

"I *cain't* do without her, Daddy," protested Frances. "I miss her so much!"

"I know, darling, and so do I," Oscar sighed.

In the middle of the second week of Elinor's absence, during an unseasonably warm week in January of 1941, the National Guardsmen received word that in two days more they would be sent down to Camp Blanding on the Atlantic coast of Florida for basic training. The boys and men had two days to put their affairs in order, to say their goodbyes, and to go out and get good and drunk.

On the afternoon of the day before they were to go off at six the following morning, two high school seniors, next-door neighbors and friends all their lives, who were now being plucked from the middle of their schooling and their infatuations with girls, drove over the Florida line, and with a one-dollar bribe, purchased a case of twenty-four bottles of Budweiser beer.

Upon returning to Perdido, fearful of being seen by parents or other adults likely to be disapproving of their alcoholic indulgence, they drove around the town to the north and parked their automobile in the grove of live oaks just above the junction of the Perdido and Blackwater rivers. They immediately proceeded to open bottles and to guzzle them down. On their third round, one of the boys was overcome with the need to relieve himself. He climbed out of the car and went over to one of the live oaks. Standing there, urinating on one of the outermost drooping limbs, he caught sight of something shining and metallic within the curtain of branches and leaves. When he had buttoned up, he pushed aside the limbs and went under the living umbrella that the ancient live oak had produced. To his astonishment, he discovered an automobile. A small suitcase lay on the back seat, and the keys remained in the ignition. In his beer-befuddled state he tried to solve the mystery of the unoccupied car's presence in this spot.

His protracted absence drew his friend, but the friend could provide no explanation either. In hope of finding some clue to the owner of the vehicle, and emboldened by the consumption of three bottles of

Budweiser, the boys opened the suitcase. It was empty.

"The car's stolen," said the boy who had discovered it. "It's bound to be stolen, and the thief left it here."

"If he was just leaving it and going off, then why would he bother to hide it?" his friend asked.

"Maybe there's a body in the trunk."

Not even the thought that tomorrow they would be formally inducted into the army provided courage sufficient to test *that* hypothesis.

The boys stumbled nervously out from beneath the tree and returned to their car. They consumed four more bottles of beer in an attempt to forget about the automobile hidden under the tree, and six more than that in drunkenly trying to predict what military life would have in store for them. As the sun lowered in the sky, the boys fell unconscious in the car. They hoped to wake sober.

Early next morning three buses parked in front of the town hall, and one hundred fifteen men climbed on. Most of Perdido was there to see them off. The occasion was suddenly marred, however, by the announcement that two high school seniors were missing. No other conscripted men in all of Baldwin County had failed to appear. It was perceived as a black mark against the town that these two boys had deserted. Their parents, shamed and fretful, returned to their homes, faintly maintaining that some accident had befallen the boys; that some irreproachable necessity had kept them away.

The Caskeys had joined their fellow townspeople at the town hall, and after the buses had driven off to a lackluster cheering, they also returned home. To their immense surprise, Elinor's automobile was parked in front of her house, and Elinor herself was sitting on the front porch, waiting for them. Oscar's step quickened, as Frances actually ran toward her mother. Elinor caught her daughter in her arms, and lifted her off the ground.

"Oh, Mama, I missed you so much! We didn't know *when* you were coming back, and I looked out the window about fifty million times hoping I would see you come driving up."

"Well," laughed Elinor, "I'm back now, darling."

"You look wonderful," said Frances, somewhat surprised, as she drew back from her mother and looked carefully into her face.

Oscar and the others had reached the steps of the house by now.

"You *do* look wonderful," said Oscar. Elinor came down the steps and kissed her husband. Everyone fought for the opportunity to hug her.

"I *feel* wonderful," said Elinor. "I feel like I could take on the whole German army."

"It looks like this trip did you a world of good," said James.

"What'd you do up in Wade, Mama?" asked Frances.

"Nothing. Not a single thing. I just went home and sat around. I didn't do a thing in the world. I was just so glad to get rid of all of you for two weeks, that's all." She laughed merrily. Oscar wondered how long it had been since he had heard his wife so light-hearted.

"How was your family?" asked Sister.

"Oh, fine," replied Elinor vaguely. "There's not many of them left, and we don't get along so well anymore."

"Why not?" asked Grace.

"Oh, because they think I went off and deserted them when I came down here and married Oscar, that's why. Most of 'em never leave home, and I was one of 'em who did. They got mad, that's all."

"Are they still mad?" asked Oscar curiously. Elinor had *never* spoken of her family.

"Of course," she returned with a smile. "But for two weeks, I didn't care. They could say whatever they wanted. I was just glad to be home for a while."

Elinor seemed to have regained all her energy and drive. Now she was never still, she was never unhappy, and she was never without some project or other. She set Bray to building up a new camellia bed in the back of the house, despite his protestation that nothing would grow in the sand. She bought new furniture for the downstairs rooms. She ran up curtains for the second floor of Miriam and Sister's house without their having said they needed them. She talked to Oscar ceaselessly about the coming war's probable effect on business, and she drove all around the county knocking on doors and asking if anyone needed employment at the mill. She sometimes went with Frances and Miriam to Mobile and shopped all day while they were in school. She and Zaddie cleaned the house, and threw out everything that hadn't been used in the past two years. She drove Leo Benquith out to the Sapps and made him examine and treat every one of the Sapp children and grandchildren for the diseases that were common to impoverished country families. She went with Queenie to visit Dollie Faye Crawford out on the Bay Minette road. She offered to teach Lucille how to sew on a machine. She made fruitcakes to send to Malcolm who was stationed in New Jersey. Her high spirits seemed to infect the whole family.

The news from Europe grew worse and worse, and the War Department placed more and more orders with Oscar's office. For the first time since 1926 the Caskey mill operated at near capacity. Beneath all life in Perdido there was a low-pitched hum of activity. It might have been the mill machinery cutting lumber and chips, fashioning poles and posts, doorjambs and window frames. Or it might have been the Perdido, nearly forgotten behind its walls of red clay, spilling along with its old urgency, its old inexorability, tumbling leaves and sticks and bones down to the junction, and burying them in the mud at the bottom of the river.

The one hundred fifteen Perdido boys finished basic training late in April, and then were scattered around the country. Most ended up in Michigan, some in Missouri, and a few were sent to help in the building of Camp Rucca. The two high school seniors were never found. A week after they were to have left for basic training, however, their automobile, with a half case of unopened Budweiser beer in the back, was discovered in the grove of live oaks on the uninhabited side of the junction.

CHAPTER 49

Rationing

Lucille and Queenie didn't even know where Pearl Harbor was when they heard the news over the radio on Sunday afternoon; few people in Perdido did. Everyone, though, knew what the Japanese bombing meant to the country. All afternoon people went from house to house, and said things like: "I wonder what's gone come of us now." War was indisputable. How Perdido would be affected was a much-discussed question.

Three days after the declaration of war, gasoline was rationed. Because of their ownership of an industry considered vital to the defense of the nation, each of the Caskey households was awarded a "C" classification, entitling them to fifteen gallons of gasoline a week. Sugar rationing followed in short order. Later, shoes and meat were placed under containment. All citizens were required to register at the town hall in order to receive their coupons, and revelation of age was necessary. The privacy of Perdido women had never been so infringed upon before, and despite the pleas for patriotism, not one admitted to years beyond fifty-five—even those who frequently had been heard to draw up some remembrance of the Civil War.

With a sudden bound, the country's economy was on its feet again, as Oscar had predicted. The office of the Caskey mill was filled with defense orders. Frances and Miriam, on Saturdays and Sundays, went to the mill to help their father sort through his work. Frances was as much hindrance as help, but Miriam understood the business instinctively, though she had rarely even visited the mill. In one of the company trucks—so as not to waste their personal allotment of gasoline—Elinor and Queenie drove through the countryside, stopping every man they saw and offering him work at the Caskey mills.

All the new military bases were being constructed of wood. At Camp Rucca three thousand men were living in tents. Barracks needed to be raised as quickly as possible. Oscar often was able to deliver lumber on the day after it was formally requested. Eglin Field, down near Pensacola, had begun its expansion. Oscar got that contract, too. Thousands of miles of electric lines were being strung across the country, and Oscar's plant manufactured utility poles quicker and better than anyone else.

Oscar was devilishly busy. He had not only to cope with mounting paperwork, but had to learn to deal with the military. This was quite different from his previous business experience, which had been transacted with less exacting but more knowledgeable civilians. At a time when every patriotic man had enlisted, and every poor man had gone in for the twenty-one dollars a month with room and board, and every other man had been drafted, Oscar sought workers to staff a second shift. He made inspection tours of the Caskey forests to determine order of cutting; and because he knew more about the matter than anyone else, he had to supervise replanting.

Life in Perdido changed quickly. There was now full employment, and the mill ached for more workers. Many of the women in town found employment building Liberty ships at the shipyards in Pensacola and Mobile. Every morning at six o'clock, two buses left from the town hall filled with excited Perdido wives who never had held jobs. There was intense activity wholly unprecedented in this quiet corner of rural Alabama. So much money came in from the defense contracts that Oscar saw fit to raise salaries across the board twice in the first six months of the war. The workers shared their newfound income with Perdido. Stores that had closed at the beginning of the Depression opened again and instantly thrived.

Even Baptist Bottom saw improvement. Black men worked at the mill or had joined the army. Black women took over the running of white households where husband and wife were both off working. Black girls as young as thirteen were pressed into responsible service.

From the beginning, Oscar made money. He had not anticipated that prosperity would be dependent upon the declaration of war, but nevertheless the Caskey mills *were* prepared, and in that readiness there was considerable profit.

Sister and James no longer had to come to Oscar for pin money. With increasing frequency, Oscar presented his uncle and his sister with checks for several hundred dollars. Later he was giving them several thousands. James and Sister stared at the drafts, and endorsed them with surprised and shaky hands.

"Oscar," said Sister at dinner one evening, "when I was little, and then when I was living with Early, I didn't know much about the mill. Nobody would ever tell me a thing. But we never made money like this, did we? Mama had it piled up and stashed away,

87

I know, but it never came in this quick and easy, did it? Every time I turn around you are handing me a check."

James replied to Sister, "No, it *never* came this easy or this fast. And it's not just the war either. It's what Oscar did *before* the war. Oscar, did you know all this was gone happen?"

"Sort of," said Oscar with a little discomfort. "I knew *something* was gone happen. Actually, the one to thank is Elinor."

Elinor nodded a small acknowledgment of her husband's praise.

"What'd *you* do?" asked Sister.

"Elinor was always at me to expand the plant, to get things set up right, even when I was reaching into capital to do it. It took something for me to get over that—you know how Mama was about people using their capital. Expand, improve, build up, get new equipment, buy more land—Elinor just harped and harped on me about it."

Sister and James turned to Elinor. "Then you knew about the war."

"No," said Elinor as if she really didn't mean it. "I just knew what was right for Oscar and the mill."

"We are getting rich, I'm telling y'all that right now," Oscar went on. "And what's making us rich is that we have all that land. Every time five acres came up for sale Elinor was on to me about it. She'd say, 'Oscar, go get it.' And I'd do it, just to shut her up. You know, there's those mills up in Atmore and Brewton, and if they had the trees they could get the contracts like I do. But they don't have trees, and every time an order comes in they got to go pretty far afield, they got to go *looking* for timber. In the last ten years they've been cutting back, they even sold some of their land to me, and now they're being brought up short. They all thought I was crazy to sink money into land."

"I thought you were crazy, too," admitted James.

"Yes," nodded Sister. "But you and Elinor proved James and me wrong, thank goodness. There have been times when I wasn't sure I was gone be able to pay Miriam's schooling."

"Good Lord, Sister," said James, "in another couple of months, we're gone have enough money to buy that whole damn college..."

Queenie Strickland's friendship with Dollie Faye Crawford had been sincere; she had not sought it only in order to assure favorable testimony when Malcolm's case came to trial. After Malcolm had gone away to join the army, Queenie's visits to the country store continued, and Queenie began shopping there, as did James and Elinor. It was an unheard of thing for the richest family in town to stock its pantry out of a ramshackle little place out in the country, but the Caskeys didn't care for Perdido's opinion. The family wanted to continue to make up for the shock Dollie Faye had suffered when confronted by Malcolm Strickland and Travis Gann with shot guns.

As a result of this new and somewhat extraordinary clientele, Dollie Faye stocked better merchandise. With money from James Caskey, she built a smokehouse out in back; she soon added a slaughterhouse, and got the son of a neighboring farmer to preside over its operations. Other Perdido residents made the trek out to the store on the Bay Minette road when it became known that Mrs. Crawford supplied the best bacon and pork in the county. Elinor lent Dollie Faye a thousand dollars. Oscar sent over four carpenters for a week's work making improvements on the store.

Dollie Faye was aware that the Caskeys were the source of her newfound prosperity, and she made sure, despite rationing, that they never suffered. She made surreptitious telephone calls each time a hog was about to be slaughtered, and Queenie or Elinor or Sister was out at the store in time to hear the pig squealing. Sugar was so plentiful for the Caskeys that Elinor continued to make her fruitcakes. Sugar, in any case, would have been no problem, for Ivey and Zaddie and Luvadia had as much cane sugar as they wanted from their mother's farm out beyond the Old Federal Road. Dollie Faye had trouble only with shoes and with tires. Oscar could usually manage the latter with his newly formed connections with the military, and occasionally, in the company of a colonel or two, he was allowed to make purchases at the military provision stores on the Eglin base, and bought shoes there.

When the war began, Early Haskew was hired by the War Department as a civilian engineer. He was given a substantial salary and immediately sent to Washington. He telephoned Sister to tell her this news. She was genuinely happy for Early. She had been separated from her husband for so long that she now thought of him like an old friend. The news of an old friend obtaining a lucrative and important position pleased her. She was also happy that the transfer was taking Early just that much farther away. In his official capacity, he got hold of extra ration coupons, stuck them in envelopes and mailed them to Sister. The Caskeys were well provided for in this time that proved difficult and tragic for so many.

In fact, Perdido as a whole suffered less than many parts of the country. The town was scarcely out of the Depression yet, and many of the boys who went off to the army did so with a willingness exceeding duty to country. Sustenance and shelter and pocket money were surer things in a uniform in Michigan than they were in a falling-down forest shack in rural Baldwin County. Much of the land around Perdido was Caskey forest, but there were small farmers here and there, some black, some Indian, some impoverished white—people who resented governmental attempts to regulate any part of their lives. Their animals were slaughtered in private, their crops gathered in the first hours of the morning before agents were likely to be out on the road. In answering those agents' questions, the farmers would protest that bad weather, insects, and marauding animals had decimated their crops. Their dirt-streaked children sold vegetables out of mule wagons driven slowly along the residential streets of Perdido. Out of sight in a closed box were slabs of bacon, beef steaks wrapped in brown paper, and chickens with wrung necks.

The Caskeys feared that, because of the curtailment of gasoline to civilians, Miriam and Frances would have to move into the dormitories of Sacred Heart. The family pooled their allotments of coupons so that, with care, the two daughters might finish out at least the remainder of the semester. Miriam would then graduate, and the question become moot for her; but Frances, returning to school the following autumn, would have to resign herself to leaving her home.

One chilly morning early in March, half an hour before the sun had risen, Miriam and Frances were driving out of Perdido, on their way to seven-thirty classes. As they neared Crawford's store, Miriam said, "Frances, isn't that Miz Crawford standing out in front of her store with a lantern?" Frances roused herself from her usual reverie, peered ahead, and replied, "Sure is. Slow down."

In the darkness, Miriam pulled up in the red clay drive of the store.

"Hey, Miz Crawford," said Frances, "is there something wrong?"

"No, ma'am," replied Dollie Faye. "I just thought you might be low on gas this morning."

"We can get to Mobile and back," said Miriam. "And I didn't bring any coupons."

"Let me fill it up for you," said Dollie Faye, taking the nozzle from the pump. "You can give me the coupon some other time."

"Hey, Mr. Crawford," said Frances, waving at Dial. The old man slumped up off the bench and came forward with a wet rag to wipe off the windshield.

Dial Crawford stared at her and mumbled incoherently.

"Sir?" asked Frances, not understanding a word he said.

"Don't mind him," called Dollie Faye from the back of the car. "You be quiet, Dial!"

The man continued to murmur and stare at Frances all the while he wiped the windshield. Something about him frightened Frances, and she drew her sweater closer about her shoulders.

After filling the tank, Dollie Faye came around and said, "I'll put it on Sister's bill."

"Thank you, Miz Crawford," said Miriam politely. "I'll drop the coupons by tomorrow."

"Well," said Dollie Faye, with some significance, "don't worry about it. You two girls save your brains for school. I know how hard you're working down there, and it makes your family so happy. Listen, you need any gas, you stop by here on your way down in the morning. Just knock on my window there"— she pointed behind her—"and I'll get up and give it to you." She looked up and down the road. It was dark, and no car had passed since Miriam had pulled up. "There's never anybody out this early..."

Miriam said, "Miz Crawford, you just got yourself a pair of wings in heaven."

With a full tank of gas, Miriam and Frances drove off through the darkness toward Mobile.

* * *

With Dollie Faye's undercover assistance, Miriam and Frances finished their year at Sacred Heart. Miriam graduated second in her class, and the Caskeys were all there to see her accept her diploma. Miriam did not hesitate to declare herself relieved that it was all over and done with now. Back in Perdido, no one dared ask her the question, What will you do now? And characteristically, Miriam did not immediately reveal her intentions. Instead, the day after graduation she appeared at breakfast at her parents' house and said to her father, "Well, Oscar, since I'm not going to Mobile today, I might as well go over to the mill and help you out."

"Lord, Miriam, I wish you would. I sure could use some help. Every day it seems like I'm getting further and further behind in everything."

Father and daughter drove off together, came home at noon together, went back to the mill together right after second glasses of iced tea, and collapsed on the front porch together at five-thirty. "Miriam," her father said with a shaking of his head, "you went through that work like nobody's business. I never saw anything like it. You've set me up for a week."

"I'll go again tomorrow if you want me," said Miriam offhandedly. "I don't have anything else to do yet."

"I wish you would," returned Oscar quickly. He had not dared ask her directly.

After that, Miriam went to the mill every day. She kept the same hours as her father. Oscar had a hole knocked in one wall of his office in order to double the space. Miriam got her own desk and filing cabinets, and found a high school girl to do her typing. A month later, Oscar came to her office, and handed her a paycheck.

"Oscar," she said, looking at the draft, "why are

you wanting to pay me for this work? I'm doing it for fun."

"I cain't help it, Miriam. I was feeling so guilty about you working your head off like you're doing, I have to do it to ease my conscience."

She looked at the check. "Then I guess I really am working for you."

"That's right. I don't think I could do without you now."

"I don't think you could either," she confirmed. She handed her father the check across the desk. "So this isn't enough money. Raise my salary."

He shook his head, sighed, and wandered off to the accounting office. Miriam got her raise.

"What are you gone do with all that money, darling?" Sister asked her one evening at Elinor's.

"None of your business," returned Miriam. Only Miriam could have said that without true insolence.

"Are you gone give me some to help run the house?"

Miriam laughed. "Sister, you are rich as Croesus right now. Are you gone give me some rent for living over there in the house that belongs to me?"

"No," returned Sister, "I am not. You don't have any idea how much time and energy I put in to keeping that house going."

"Then we're even," retorted Miriam. She looked around the porch at her family, the members of which were reading, playing checkers, or rocking in swings and gliders in the warm evening breezes. "I'm investing my money," Miriam said.

"In what?" asked Frances, looking up.

"Diamonds," returned Miriam. "I got me another safety-deposit box, and I'm gone fill it up..."

The family concluded that Miriam would always be Mary-Love's little girl, no matter *how* long the old woman had been dead.

CHAPTER 50

Billy Bronze

Every Saturday and Sunday throughout the duration of the war, Perdido was flooded with soldiers on leave from Eglin Air Base. Some of these men wanted to attend church and others wanted to find a local girl to take to the dance hall built on stilts out over Lake Pinchona. These soldiers were eagerly taken in by Perdido families, given massive plates of fish on Saturday night, hams and racks of ribs on Sunday after church, and entertained on the front porch afterward. The servicemen were admitted free to the Ritz Theater and lent automobiles for drives to the lake. In return, the people of Perdido got extra ration coupons, smuggled tires, and food no longer available in the stores. Perdido remembered how the town had been changed by the influx of levee workers back in '22, and this wasn't all that different, except that the men were in uniform, came from all parts of the country, and were—thank God!—much more polite.

At the end of every Sunday church service, the

congregation sang all four verses of "God Bless America" from an insert glued in the front of their hymnals. During this patriotic song, Elinor always looked about at the congregation, and would pick out the three or four or five soldiers she would ask home that day. During the postlude she would point out her choices to Queenie and Sister, and all three would hurry off to capture the men before anyone else got to them. For soldiers, Zaddie, Ivey, and Roxie fixed dinner and supper. Alone, the Caskeys had always got by with just dinner. Every Sunday, Elinor's dining room was crowded with family and the visitors in uniform. Some of the men from Eglin came only once, but most returned two or three times. Those particularly favored by the family visited the Caskeys at every conceivable opportunity. The family had never been so social or garrulous. There was always an Air Corps man worrying the cooks in the kitchen, sitting with Elinor on the porch upstairs, or waiting on the front steps for Frances and Miriam to return from Mobile late in the afternoon.

Occasionally colored servicemen came and lounged on the lattice or in the back yard, much to the delight of Zaddie and Luvadia.

Sometimes, at meals, their numbers were so large that the dining room would not hold them, and the food was served on a buffet set out on the upstairs porch. They flirted with Sister, who was older than the mothers of most of them; they treated James and Oscar with deference. They were in awe of Elinor, and studiously polite around Frances and Miriam and Lucille as if to show the complete innocence of their intentions. They tried to take Danjo hunting, and they challenged Grace to increasingly more strenuous bouts of athletic prowess.

Most of these uniformed visitors were never around long enough to form really intimate ties with the family. After a certain amount of training they were shipped out to Europe or the South Pacific. The Caskeys received a postcard or two, sometimes censored, but soon communication usually ceased.

The single exception to this transience on the part of Elinor's multitude of guests was a corporal from the North Carolina mountains. His name was Billy Bronze. He was an instructor in radio mechanics and permanently stationed at Eglin for the training of recent enlistees. He was strikingly handsome, with dark blond hair, gray eyes, and a jaw blue-shadowed with beard. His manner was reserved but self-assured. He was twenty-seven, and since most of Elinor's guests were no more than nineteen or twenty, he seemed mature in comparison. He once put a stop to some rowdiness in the back yard between white and colored soldiers and for his welcome intervention he was remembered and particularly asked back again. He came the next day, and the day after that. One weekend, he was asked to stay in one of the guest rooms if his leave and commanding officer permitted. He did so the following Saturday night. Elinor came to rely on Corporal Bronze to keep all the boys in order, to weed out troublemakers, and to recommend those lonely men at Eglin who were most likely to benefit from the Caskeys' hospitality.

Billy, in most circumstances, was straightforward and friendly; with Frances, however, he seemed shy. Despite this shyness, and Frances's natural diffidence, they sought each other's company. And there were many opportunities for them to be together. Billy came to Perdido at least two evenings a week and sometimes more often. He spent every other weekend there, sleeping in the front room. In a house bustling with family, servants, and guests, however, the two young people rarely found themselves alone.

Oscar said to his wife one Saturday night as they lay in bed after the house was quiet at last, "Corporal Bronze is paying a lot of attention to our little girl."

"Yes, I believe he is," replied Elinor.

"What do you think of that?"

"I think Billy's a fine young man."

"Is he good enough for Frances?"

"Nobody is good enough for our Frances, but she's bound to get married sometime, and Billy wouldn't be nearly as bad as some of the boys who have come through here. But it's one thing to feed them at the dinner table, and it's another to have them marry our daughter."

"Do you think we should say anything to Frances?" Oscar asked.

Elinor shook her head. "Frances will have decisions to make sometime or other. She's only twenty. Maybe she can put them off."

"Elinor, what sort of decisions are you talking about? You mean getting married?"

"No...not that," murmured Elinor vaguely. "Oscar, let's go to sleep. With these boys around, my days are always long..."

The Caskeys saw the incipient romance between Frances and Billy Bronze, but they were more curious to see how Elinor would react to it than they were to watch the actual progress of this tentative courtship. They all still remembered how Mary-Love, dead for five years now, had discouraged all relationships outside the family; she would have had everyone remain unmarried and dependent upon her if she had had her way. Elinor had taken Mary-Love's place in the family, and it seemed to them that in that role she would react just as her mother-in-law had. But Elinor did not. She made no objection. In fact, she encouraged Billy's visits warmly, saying, "Frances enjoys having you around so much. The rest of us do, too." Late on Saturday nights, after all the other boys had returned to Eglin and only Billy remained, Elinor took her husband off to bed and left Frances and Billy alone on the screened porch.

On one such night, after they had been thus thoughtfully abandoned, Billy and Frances sat next to each other in the swing, rocking slowly and fanning themselves with paper fans. The hot night wind blew through the high branches of the water oaks, and the kudzu rustled on the bank of the levee. By the hundreds, moths anchored themselves to the screens, attracted to the low lights on the porch. Frances talked about Sacred Heart, and Billy spoke of Eglin. That night he kissed her.

The following night he kissed her twice.

"Who's your family?" Frances asked.

"I just have my father," he said. "And he's old and mean. Got money, though," laughed Billy.

"Your mama's dead?"

"He killed her."

"Killed her!"

"Talked mean to her for twenty-five years, until it just wore her out. He started talking mean to me at the funeral—because she wasn't around—so I joined the Air Corps. He said, 'Don't do it, Billy, I need me somebody to talk to.' I said, 'You talk to the walls and your empty bed. Goodbye.'"

"You shouldn't have spoken to your daddy like that," said Frances reprovingly.

"He killed my mother," returned Billy simply. "It was either join the Air Corps or end up beating him over the head with a two-by-four. I would have done it, too, if he had been talking mean to me for another two minutes."

"I'm sorry you don't get along."

"I am too. That's why I like coming around here."

"Why?" asked Frances.

"Because you're such a happy family."

Frances gave a little laugh.

* * *

Danjo was seventeen and in his junior year in high school when war was declared. James Caskey prayed God every night that Danjo might not be influenced by Elinor's visiting servicemen to enlist on the day that he turned eighteen. James would have been as forlorn without Danjo as Queenie was without Malcolm—who didn't even bother to write to his mother.

"You don't want to leave me, do you, darling?" said James. They were having breakfast one morning before Danjo went to school. Grace had left an hour earlier for an early morning swim at Lake Pinchona.

" 'Course not," replied Danjo. "But probably I got to, James, unless they call off the war."

"They're not gone do that, I'm afraid. No, sir."

"I've been talking to Billy—"

"Don't you talk to those boys, Danjo, not even Billy Bronze!" cried James. "They're gone want you to join up. Bad enough they're always wanting to put a gun in your hands. Haven't Queenie and I taught you better than that? You remember what happened to your daddy and how he died. You remember what your brother did to poor old Dollie Faye Crawford. You think about that next time somebody puts a gun in your hands."

"I hate guns!" cried Danjo vehemently.

"You're my precious boy!" said James, and squeezed Danjo's hand across the table.

"Still, I was talking to Billy..." Danjo resumed tentatively.

"And?"

"James, you know I *got* to sign up next year sometime, I just *got* to."

"It's gone kill me if you do! I suppose you have to do it. This country has been so good to us, and now I guess it's time for us to be good to it. But I don't want you picking up a gun unless you are planning to shoot Adolf Hitler himself."

"I won't," promised Danjo. "Let me finish, will you? Billy said if I signed up now—"

"No!"

"—if I signed up now," repeated Danjo deliberately, "I could sort of have my choice. And what he said was I could join the Air Corps and he'd talk to people and try to get me stationed over at Eglin. I could get in the Radio Corps, and Billy would take care of me for as long as he could. See, that's all I was trying to say, James, and you wouldn't let me finish!"

"Does Billy really think he could get you stationed over at Eglin?"

"He says he could try."

James nodded slowly. "Then the next time I see him I'll speak to him about it. Maybe if you were over at Eglin, Danjo, it wouldn't kill me to have you gone."

"You'll have Grace here," Danjo pointed out.

"Grace will not make up for the loss of my little boy. Danjo, I just don't know what I'm gone do without you! I'm such an old man—I'm an old gray mare—and there's no more children around for me to steal and bring up like they were my own."

"Maybe Grace'll get married and have children, and you can take one of hers," suggested Danjo brightly.

"Grace is already an old bachelor," sighed James. "She's not gone get married. That's fine, 'cause she's pretty happy staying here with me, but I'm not gone get any grandchildren out of her."

"You want me to get married then?"

"I most certainly do not! You are too young to even think about that! I haven't even told you yet..."

"Told me what?"

James shrugged, embarrassed. "How babies get born."

"I know that!" laughed Danjo. "James, I'm seventeen, 'course I know that!"

"Who told you?"

"Grace."

James shook his head slowly. "She would have."

"Grace tells all the girls, and one day she told me, too. She's got these pictures, James, you ought to see them—"

"Don't talk about this to me at the breakfast table, Danjo. I don't want to hear it! If you know all about it already, then we don't ever have to mention it again."

"No, sir!" laughed Danjo.

Following Billy's suggestions, and with James's reluctant assent, Danjo joined the Air Corps in September of 1942, though he would not be formally inducted until the following June, when he had turned eighteen and graduated from high school. Nothing could be certain in this war, but Billy provided tentative assurances that Danjo, after three months of basic training, would find his way back to Eglin. James could not be happy, however, and thought only of the scant nine months that remained for Danjo to be at home with him.

He sighed to Grace one afternoon, "Every morning I get up and I say to myself, 'There's one less day Danjo's gone be around.'"

Grace always took the forthright and practical view of any matter. "You've still got more than half a year of him. Enjoy that, Daddy. Don't ruin it by always thinking of when he's going away. And just remember, he'll be headed back to Eglin before you know it. Two years from then he'll be a civilian again, and he'll come back here and things will be just like they always were."

"He could get killed. He could get his legs shot

off. I may be dead," protested James Caskey. "Things are never 'just like they always were' again."

Grace slapped a magazine against the arm of the glider with a crack. "Daddy," she said, "you have got to be the silliest man I ever met in my life. I don't *know* what I'm going to do with you for the rest of this war."

The efforts of Billy Bronze in the cause of keeping Danjo Strickland and James Caskey together were fully appreciated by the Caskeys. They not only liked Billy, they were now indebted to him. Elinor no longer extended invitations to him, because he only had to appear to be welcomed. He was regarded as one of the family to such an extent that his presence never restrained them from talking about private family matters. He heard details of old family enmities, and new family finances that no one in Perdido knew about. Short, testy arguments exploded in his presence, and little moments of affection were exhibited before him. He became another Caskey son, brother, uncle, and cousin.

The corporal was a favorite also of his commanding officer. He was allowed, so long as he did not abuse the privilege, of sleeping over at the Caskeys on some week nights as well as every other weekend. Oscar lent him one of their automobiles, saying that with gas rationing they had no use for it anyway. Billy Bronze came and went with ever-increasing frequency; the front room was always ready for him. Elinor, trusting both Billy and Frances implicitly, did not even bother locking the linen corridor that connected the two rooms.

One evening in the autumn of 1942—a few hours after Billy Bronze had returned to Eglin—Frances begged a private conference with her mother. *"Very private, Mama,"* she said. Elinor took her daughter down the long second-floor hallway, through the door

103

with the stained glass at the end, and out onto the narrow front porch where no one ever sat. Mother and daughter took adjoining rockers. The evening was dark. Crickets chorused in the orchard across the road. Elinor rocked steadily in her chair.

"I bet I know what you want to ask me about," she said.

"You do?"

"You want me to tell you about husbands and wives."

Frances blushed in the darkness.

"No, ma'am, not that."

Elinor paused in her rocking. "What then?"

"Dial Crawford."

Elinor laughed. "Dial Crawford? What on earth have you got to do with that old man? Poor old Dollie Faye. She told me Dial hasn't been right in his head for twenty years, and he's no more help to her than a three-year-old."

"He washes windshields."

"And not much else," confirmed Elinor. "What about Dial, darling? What on earth do you want to know about *him?*"

Frances began hesitantly: "I...stop out at Miss Dollie Faye's for gas about twice a week, on my way to school, and Mr. Crawford always washes the windshield. He always speaks, but he has such a funny voice that it was always hard for me to understand what he was saying. For a long time, I had no idea what he was talking about, but in the past month or two, it seems like I got used to the way he sounds, and I can understand him. So we always speak. Some days, even when I'm not stopping, I see him sitting out in front of the store and he stands up and waves. So I wave back. I guess he knows the car, and knows what time I'm gone be coming past."

"Well? He probably doesn't have much to occupy him."

"Mama, that's five o'clock in the morning!"

"Country people get up early. Anyway, go on, Frances."

"Yesterday morning, I had plenty of gas so I wasn't gone stop. But there was Mr. Crawford, standing on the side of the road, waving me down. So I stopped the car, and I said, 'Is there something wrong, Mr. Crawford?' So, Mama, he looks at me, and he says, '*Black water.*'"

"*Black water?*" echoed Elinor, with the same inflection.

"He said, '*Black water,* that's where you came from. *Black water,* that's where you're going back to.'" Frances glanced at her mother in the darkness, but could not determine her expression. Elinor had stopped her rocking.

"What else did Dial say, darling?"

"He said something else..."

"What?" prompted Elinor with some impatience.

"He said, 'Your mama crawled out of the river.' He said, 'Tell your mama to crawl back in and leave me alone.'"

Elinor laughed. "I didn't know I had been upsetting Dial Crawford. Maybe I ought to stay away from there from now on, and let Queenie do all my shopping for me."

"Mama, what did he mean, that you crawled out of the river?"

"Frances, Dial is a crazy old man. He doesn't know what he's saying, and Dollie Faye ought to teach him to keep his mouth shut." Frances didn't reply. "Darling, do *you* think I crawled out of the river?"

"No, no," returned Frances hastily. "Of course not. It's just that sometimes..."

"Sometimes what?"

"Sometimes I think you and I are different—different from everybody else."

"How do you mean?"

"I don't know how I mean, Mama. It's just that sometimes I feel like I'm not all here, not the way Miriam is, not the way Daddy and Sister and Queenie and everybody else is. I feel like part of me is somewhere else."

"Where is that somewhere else?"

"I don't know. I'm not sure." Frances paused. "I *do* know where else. The river, the Perdido. Just like Mr. Crawford said, *black water,* flowing out there behind the levee. And, Mama," Frances said very softly, "when I'm there, you're there too."

For a few minutes, Elinor said nothing. Then she asked, "And does this bother you?"

"No, not until yesterday, when Mr. Crawford sort of put his finger on it. When he said what he said, I realized what I had been feeling all these years."

"If you've been feeling it all these years, what difference does it make now?"

Frances didn't answer.

Elinor took her daughter's hand and squeezed it. "I know why," she whispered. She raised Frances's hand to her lips and kissed it. "It's because of Billy, isn't it, darling?"

"Yes, ma'am," replied Frances in a timid voice. "I just wanted to know if it would make a difference. If I ever wanted to get married, or anything. And the problem is, I don't even know what 'it' is."

Elinor did not reply immediately. After a few moments' silence, she said to her daughter, "Frances, I'm going to answer your question and I'm going to tell you the truth. But when I do that, I don't want any more questions, you understand?"

"Yes, ma'am."

"Then the truth is that someday, in your lifetime, it *will* make a difference. It won't make a difference now. You go ahead and do whatever you want to. Someday, Frances, I'm going to be the proudest woman in town, 'cause I'm going to watch my little

106

girl get married to a man who will make her happy. And someday my little girl is going to give me some grandchildren."

"Mama, you think so?"

"I don't think so, I *know* it." Elinor laughed then. She still had hold of Frances's hand, and she squeezed it again. "And you know what I'm going to do? I'm going to steal one of those children, just like Mary-Love stole Miriam from me. Then everybody in this family can rant and rave and say that I'm just as bad as Mary-Love ever was. But I'll have me a little girl..."

"How do you know it'll be a girl?"

Elinor didn't answer. She seemed only happy in anticipating the stealing of a grandchild. She reassured Frances: "I don't want you to be thinking about what Dial Crawford said to you, you hear? It's not going to make any difference for a long, long time."

"But someday it will?"

"No questions, I told you! But someday...yes, it will. Darling, I promise you I'll be there when that time comes. And when the time comes, I'll tell you what you need to know. You believe that?"

"Yes, ma'am."

"You trust me, Frances?"

"Yes, ma'am."

"You are my little girl. Miriam isn't. Even if I hadn't given Miriam away to Mary-Love, and had kept both of you, you'd still be my daughter in a way that Miriam is not."

Frances was obediently silent, and asked no further questions.

Elinor's voice grew faraway. "I had a sister. Bet you didn't know that..."

"No, ma'am. You've never mentioned her," said Frances cautiously. Hoping that they did not constitute forbidden questions, she asked: "Is she still alive? What was her name?"

"My mama had two daughters. My sister was just like my mama, but I wasn't anything like my mama. My mama said to me, 'Elinor, you're so different, you go off and do whatever you want. I have'"—Elinor paused as if her sister's name had escaped her memory. In a moment she resumed—"'I have Nerita, and Nerita is just like me in every way.' So Mama got rid of me, the way I got rid of Miriam. And Mama and Nerita were alike the way you and I are alike, do you understand that?"

"I think so."

"You see," Elinor went on, "as soon as Miriam was born, I saw that she wasn't anything like me. She was a Caskey baby, and that's why I gave her up to Mary-Love and Sister—because she belonged to them anyway. But when you were born, I saw right away that you were *my* baby, and that's why I will never give you up. I will always be here for you."

"Mama," cried Frances, "I love you so much!"

"You are my precious girl!"

Frances stumbled out of her rocker and fell at her mother's feet. She grasped her legs and squeezed them tight. Elinor leaned over and kissed her daughter's head. "Darling," she whispered in Frances's ear, "crazy old men like Dial, sometimes they know more than everybody else put together. Sometimes they speak the truth."

CHAPTER 51

~~~~~~

The Proposal

As Danjo prepared to go away for basic training at Camp Blanding on the Atlantic coast of Florida, James fussed about the boy relentlessly, wanting him in sight every minute. Most boys Danjo's age would have quickly resented an old man's worrisome solicitude, but Danjo bore with it. The last few days when he ought to have been going around town paying farewell calls, Danjo was allowed only to sit on the front porch with James and listen to the old man sigh and say things like: "I sure hope I'm alive when you get back, Danjo. I sure hope there's somebody here to open your letters when you write home."

The unhappy day of departure came at last. James had wanted Bray to drive him and Danjo the four hundred miles to Camp Blanding so that he could hug his boy at the front gate, but Danjo drew the line at this. "I'm taking the bus, James, just like everybody else does. You want to do something for me, you get Elinor to make me some candy to take along and remind me of Perdido."

The box of candy, cookies, and cakes Elinor prepared for Danjo under James's supervision weighed nearly as much as all the boy's luggage.

On the afternoon of the day before Danjo was to leave, James and his daughter sat on the front porch of their house. "Daddy," said Grace, "why are we just sitting here moping? Why don't we at least go on over to Elinor's where there's some people?"

"Grace, you go on. This afternoon, I want you to let me mope in peace."

"I don't know if I ought to point this out, Daddy, but you are making me feel real bad, going on about Danjo like this."

"Why, darling?"

"Because you act like you're left all alone. But you're not. I'm here, and haven't I sworn up and down the churchyard steeple that I'm never gone get married or leave you?"

"You have."

"Then why do you act like you are all alone in the world?"

The afternoon was hot, and James sat in his shirtsleeves. His chair was placed in the shadows of the porch so that no one passing by chance in front of the house should see him in such dishabille. He fanned himself with a paper fan. Grace sat beside him, full in the sunlight, with her arms turned outward for an even tan. Across the road, the cows in the orchard lay in the shade of the pecan trees, swishing their tails against flies.

"Let me ask you, darling," said James. "You remember how you loved all those girls who used to come and visit you here in the summers?"

" 'Course I do."

"You remember, though, when you went off to Spartanburg, you sort of got to love one girl special?"

"I do, and then she up and married and I never want to hear her name spoken aloud by you or anybody else in this town!"

"I'd never do that," returned James calmly. "Well, that's how I feel about Danjo, darling, that's how much I love that boy. I love you too, of course, I always have loved you, but Danjo's been something special to me, 'cause he was the only thing I ever had that was all my very own."

"What about me?"

"You belonged to Genevieve some. Genevieve could have taken you away from me if she had wanted to. Nobody was gone take Danjo away, not after Carl died, anyway. Are you mad at me for feeling like this?"

Grace laughed. Her eyes were closed against the sun. "Of course not, Daddy! I was just trying to get you upset, that's all. I know how you care about Danjo, and I'm not jealous. Danjo's the sweetest boy in the world, and there's nothing more to be said about *him!* I just hope you're not gone try to send me away."

"I wouldn't send my little girl away, not for the world!"

Contrary to James Caskey's doubts, Danjo Strickland was assigned to Eglin Air Base at the end of his basic training. James knew of many families who had sent their sons off with every expectation of Private X seeing two years of duty behind the information desk at the Arlington National Cemetery, only to discover that the War Department conceived that the only place for Private X was stoking the boiler of a destroyer in the western Pacific. But in Danjo's case, things worked out as planned, and after basic training, Danjo Strickland was sent to Eglin. He was able to visit his uncle two or three times a week.

Billy Bronze got all the credit for Danjo's assignment so close to home. It was true that Billy had asked his commanding officer if anything might be done, but he had no way of knowing whether his request had had anything to do with the matter. Danjo trained as a radio engineer and, as such, was under Billy's supervision. When Billy drove from Eglin over to Perdido, he often managed to bring Danjo with him, and thus his arrival in Perdido was now doubly welcome. Billy wasn't loath to accept the thanks of the Caskeys. He intended to ask Frances to marry him, and he didn't think it would hurt his cause to have the family think he had done them all a great favor.

Billy Bronze was a handsome, intelligent man, whose one desire in life was to be comfortable and to be taken care of. His father was rich, but the old man had anything but a loving disposition, and Billy had never had much comfort or care as a child. He had been packed off to military school at the age of eight. Unlike most of his young classmates, he had never allowed himself to suffer a moment of homesickness, and had never once looked forward to a holiday.

Now, years later, he was grateful for having fallen in with the Caskeys. Men at Eglin occasionally chided him for courting an heiress, and Billy, because he himself was heir to a substantial fortune, did not bridle at the accusation. He was fascinated by the Caskeys, and by the women particularly. Billy had been around few women. His mother had been a browbeaten invalid. Billy had seen her leave her shuttered room only once, and that was when she was taken from it in her coffin. His father's servants had all been men except for the cook in the kitchen, where he was never allowed. At military school he had met one woman, the wife of the commander, and one girl, the commander's daughter. Billy was one of three hundred boys, and that didn't lend itself to intimacy with those two females.

But not only were there a great many Caskey women, the women were in control of the family. Billy had never seen anything like it, and the whole notion fascinated him. He loved being around the Caskeys, and had grown very quickly to love them all. With equal delight he attended to Queenie's detailed gossip, Miriam's snide remarks, Frances's shy speech, Grace's masculine banter, Lucille's flirtatious coyness, and Elinor's commanding pronouncements. Even the servants seemed to have been affected by the Caskey women's assumption of power. Zaddie, Ivey, Roxie, and Luvadia did and said what they saw fit to do and say. In contrast, Oscar seemed rather put upon, and might have been utterly powerless if he had not enjoyed at least superficial control of the mill. James Caskey had abdicated his rights entirely, and had become a kind of woman himself. Danjo was a strong, masculine boy, but one trained nevertheless to believe that real power and real prestige lay with women and not with men. Billy, a year before he had come to Eglin, would never have believed that such a family existed. Now, he wanted never to leave them.

He wondered what he would have done if there had been no marriageable daughter in the family; by what subterfuge he would have remained in Perdido and in the Caskey circle. As it was, there were— in theory, at any rate—three such prospects in the household: Frances, Miriam, and Lucille. Lucille was out; even his limited exposure to women had taught Billy enough to know to stay away from *that* type. When it came to Miriam and Frances, so unlike each other considering that they were sisters, Billy had chosen Frances. He had made this choice not because he believed that Frances would make the better wife, but because he had thought her more likely to accept an offer of marriage. His principal aim had been to join the Caskey clan; the means by which he accomplished this was a matter of secondary importance.

So Billy wooed Frances as best he knew how—in a simple, straightforward manner. He had made it clear from the beginning that he intended sooner or later to ask her to marry him; no other method ever occurred to him. And despite his less than romantic intentions, he discovered in the course of this courtship that he actually did love Frances. He couldn't point to any particular physical, emotional, or mental attributes that made him fall in love with her; it had simply happened. And he could pinpoint the very moment. It was late one afternoon in the spring of 1943. He and Frances were walking around the house looking at the buds on the azaleas, and she was talking about the three years she had spent in bed with crippling arthritis. Suddenly he saw Frances with different eyes, as if a changed sun poured down a new quality of light upon her face and form. Interrupting her casual tale, he said, "Frances, you know what?"

"What?"

"I'm in love with you, that's what."

"You are?" she laughed, blushing. "Well, you know what? I'm in love with you, and now you and me and the whole town know it."

"The whole town?"

Frances nodded. "Every morning Queenie comes over here and she says, 'Frances, when is that boy going to ask you to marry him?'" She stopped, and laughed again. "Oh, Lord! I guess I shouldn't say that, should I? 'Cause it sounds like I'm sort of asking you to ask me."

They were in back of the house now, strolling among the slender trunks of the water oaks. They sat down on the plank seat between two of the trees.

"You want me to ask you?" Billy said.

"Well, of course I do," said Frances. "But not if you don't want to. I mean"—she stopped, and tried to look serious and upset—"I really *shouldn't* say this. Sister would kill me. Mama would probably kill me, too. I mean, if you don't want to marry me, then I'm embarrassing you, right? You'll feel sort of obligated to ask, and there won't be any way for you to get out of it. And anyway, the girl's never supposed to mention it before the boy does. But the trouble is, I'm always thinking about it, and I'm always sort of assuming it's going to happen, but I guess I shouldn't, should I? I mean, if you want to turn around and drive right back to Eglin and pretend I never said—"

"Frances, are you gone marry me or not?"

"Of course I am!" she giggled. She looked around the yard and was quiet for a moment. Then she said, "Is that it? Does that take care of everything?" Coyness, it was evident, was not to be found in Frances's repertoire of behavior.

"For the time being."

"What else is there?" asked Frances.

"Well, for one thing, we have to decide when we're going to tell your family."

"My family already knows. I told you, they keep wanting to know if you've asked me yet."

"Then we have to decide when."

"When what?"

"When we get married. I imagine your mama will want to do a little something in the way of a wedding. You're graduating from Sacred Heart in May, and we ought to wait for that. It might even be best to wait till after the war. I could be transferred out of Eglin any day."

"I don't care," said Frances. "One way or the other. I'm just glad it's all settled so I don't have to think about it anymore, and everybody will shut up about it."

115

"And the most important thing..."

"What?"

"What we're going to do after we *are* married."

Frances looked at him blankly.

"I mean," said Billy, "where we're going to live and all that."

"Oh," said Frances, as if she had not considered this before. "I don't think Mama's gone want me to move out. I think she's just gone want you to move in. Mama and Daddy would want everything to be the same except that you and I would be sleeping in the same room." A thought suddenly occured to her. She looked at Billy earnestly, and spoke with a tremor in her voice, "Billy, promise me one thing."

"What?"

"After we're married, you sleep in my room. Promise me you won't make me sleep in the front room."

He smiled. "Do you have nightmares in that room, too?"

She nodded. Then her expression changed and she said, "But wait, where do *you* want to live after we're married? I guess, if you made me, I'd go away with you."

"No, I'm not gone make you do anything you don't want to do. Besides, I want to live here. I want to move in with your mama and daddy. You know," he said, leaning over and kissing her, "that the only reason I'm marrying you is so that I can become a Caskey, too."

"I know that. I'm just lucky you didn't choose Miriam..."

They sat on the bench and stared at the levee. Suddenly, after so many weeks together in which neither had had the least difficulty with speech, both were tongue-tied.

"Let's go up there," said Frances suddenly, pointing.

"Up on the levee?"

"Yes. Haven't you ever been up at the top?"

Billy shook his head. "I didn't know you could get up there."

"Over behind James's house there are steps. The kudzu's pretty much covered them, but they're still there." She took his hand and led him across the yards to the base of the steps. They were hidden, but she had no difficulty in finding them. "Be careful," she said, "Daddy always said there're snakes living in this kudzu, even though I've never seen any."

Wading up through the kudzu as they might have maneuvered an unfamiliar staircase in the dark, they climbed to the top of the levee. In the twenty years since these clay banks had been built, the sides had been completely grown over with the rampaging vine; it had choked out everything else. But at the level top of the levee were oak and pine saplings that had taken root. Wild verbena also grew here, as well as Indian paintbrush, pale petunias, and degenerate phlox, all wind-seeded from some Perdido garden. In two decades the levee had grown almost invisible to the inhabitants of the town, even to those who lived within its very shadow. Children, to whom it was no novelty, felt no desire to play on it, and were no longer warned against its dangers. The rivers that flowed behind the levees had become even less familiar to those who lived in the town. Who ever thought of the Perdido and the Blackwater? One saw them only when crossing the bridge below the Osceola Hotel, and the new concrete sides to that bridge cut off most of that view.

At the top, Billy Bronze was surprised by the aspect of the river on the other side. "It looks so wild!" he exclaimed. The Perdido was swift, the water swirling, muddy, red. Its movement was urgent, insistent, inexorable. "It looks dangerous. No wonder they put these levees up."

Frances chuckled. "I love this river! Let's walk

down toward the junction." She took his hand and led him on. To their right were the houses that had once belonged to the DeBordenaves and the Turks. One was shut up with the windows boarded over, and the other had been taken over by the undertaker. "You know," said Frances, "Mama loves the river even more than I do. From about March till November, she swims in it every day."

"In that!?"

Frances nodded. "She's done it for as long as I can remember. Mama's about the best swimmer I ever met. I'm pretty good myself. Sometimes," Frances added with pride, "I go swimming with her."

"But it's so swift! How can you swim in it?"

Frances shrugged. "I don't know, I just do. When I was so sick," she said, with an effort to remember, "Mama bathed me every day in Perdido water and that's what finally made me well."

"How could that cure you?"

"I don't know. Mama says I was baptized in Perdido water and that's why it cured me. Maybe that was it."

They had reached the junction. Behind them was the town hall. The bus from the Pensacola shipyards was just then letting out the women workers in the parking lot; some of their husbands waited in automobiles. In front of the newly affianced couple the swift red water of the Perdido and the black water of the smaller Blackwater spiraled together and sank in a swirling vortex down toward the muddy bottom.

"When you go swimming, aren't you afraid of that?" Billy asked, pointing down.

Frances didn't answer. She stared at the whirlpool, again as if trying to remember something.

"What if you got sucked down in it? You'd be drowned for sure."

"No..." said Frances absently. "Not really."

"What do you mean?"

118

"I'm trying to remember..."

"Remember what?"

"I *have* been down there," she said at last, and looked at her fiancé with a puzzled expression. "I think I remember going down in it."

Billy looked at it again. "You'd remember that," he said.

Frances shook her head. "No...it's just vague."

"Then tell me what's down there?" Billy asked, as if it were all a tease.

"Mama..."

"What?"

"Mama's down there."

"Frances, are you all right, you look so..."

Frances shook herself, and closed her eyes tightly. She opened them and said, "Billy, I'm sorry, what were you saying?"

"Nothing. Let's go back, all right?"

They retraced their steps along the levee, and spoke no more of Frances's memory of the vortex at the junction of the rivers. They walked carefully down the steps through the kudzu. At the bottom, Billy said, "Oh, Frances, you never *really* went down that whirlpool. You couldn't have, you'd have been drowned for sure."

Frances wasted no time in telling her family of her engagement. Elinor kissed her daughter and then kissed Billy Bronze, and said, "Billy, I hope there's not going to be any nonsense about the two of you going away anywhere once you're married. I hope that you and Frances are going to want to stay on here just like you always have. What would Oscar and I do without our little girl? What would we do without *you* for that matter?"

"Elinor," said her husband, "you know who you sound like? You sound just like Mama when you and

I wanted to get married. She didn't want us to go off—and you know what kind of trouble that caused."

"Oscar, I am nothing in the world like Mary-Love, and I don't appreciate your saying I am."

"Miz Caskey," said Billy, "Frances and I aren't going anywhere. One big reason I'm marrying her in the first place is so that I can stay on here with you and Oscar."

Elinor nodded her approval of this sentiment, and Oscar looked pleased.

They sat on the upstairs porch until suppertime, talking over plans for the couple's future. One by one the other Caskeys wandered over and received the news with only slightly varying degrees of enthusiasm.

Sister's congratulations were effusive for her niece, though strangely commingled with some dismal predictions for the marriage itself. "Are you sure you know what you're getting into? I'll bet you don't. I'll bet you discover on the inside of six months that it was all a big mistake." Everyone—including Frances and Billy—understood that Sister was talking about her own marriage more than anything else, and so accepted the comments in good part.

"What about your daddy?" asked Queenie Strickland, who always found the one question no one else had thought of.

"Why, yes," said Elinor, "you think he'll come down for the wedding?"

Billy shook his head doubtfully. "No, ma'am, I don't believe he will."

"You don't think he'd approve of your marrying our little gitchee-gumee?" asked Oscar gleefully.

"Daddy, I wish you wouldn't call me that. I'm twenty-one years old. I'm not a baby, and you don't read me poems out of books anymore."

"My father," said Billy, "is pretty much bound to object to anything I do."

120

"That's too bad," said Sister sympathetically, recalling the similar aspects of her childhood.

"Is that going to stop you?" asked Elinor. "He could disinherit you."

"He could, but I don't think he'd do that. Even if he did, it wouldn't stop me."

Frances looked around the porch with pride, as if to say, *Look what this man would do for me...*

"You want me to call him up and speak to him?" asked Elinor. "I don't mind explaining things to him."

Billy shook his head. "Better let me do that. He's not going to like it—and there's no reason for you to have to listen to what he's going to say."

"I don't know why *some* people don't just up and die," said Queenie pointedly. "It would sure make some *other* people real happy."

"Queenie," said James, "you are talking about Billy's *daddy!*"

"That's all right, Mr. James," said Billy. "Mrs. Strickland's not saying any worse then I've said once or twice in my life."

"How children survive their parents," sighed Sister, "is a thing I will *never* understand."

Miriam, who through all this had sat on the glider reading the afternoon Mobile paper in the fading sunlight, folded the paper, dropped it on the floor, and said, "When is the wedding? If I'm supposed to be in it, then somebody tell me now so that I can get Sister to start thinking about getting me a dress and shoes and whatever else it takes."

"Miriam," cried Sister, "you're not supposed to ask somebody if you're going to be in their wedding, they're supposed to ask you!"

"Miriam, would you be my maid of honor?" asked Frances timidly, glancing at her mother for approval.

Elinor nodded.

"If you want me to," said Miriam. "If you don't

want me to, Frances, then say so and ask somebody else. It's not going to hurt my feelings."

"No," said Frances. "I want you. You're my sister."

"All right, then," said Miriam. "It's settled. Sister, are you gone see about getting me a dress or something to wear?"

"Well, of course I will, darling, but it's not as easy as that. First we've got to find out what the bride is going to wear. These things take a lot of time."

Miriam appeared to take the news of her sister's engagement with equanimity, if not actual indifference. "When is this thing going to be?" she asked.

"We don't know," said Billy. "At least not until after Frances finishes Sacred Heart. We may even wait till the end of the war."

"Who knows when that's going to be," snorted James. "When they've taken away *all* our boys, I guess."

"I guess," said Billy.

"You better not wait till the end of the war," said Elinor. "James is right. Who knows how long it might go on?"

Zaddie appeared in the doorway to announce supper. There was general movement as everyone got up out of swing, chair, and glider.

"Get married in the summer," said Queenie, walking toward the door.

"Not in August," said Sister, following along. "Everybody in the church will melt. And do you know what happens to flowers in a church in August? Only thing worse than to get married in August is to die in August. Mama died in August, and we had to do everything but pack her in ice."

They all headed down the stairs toward the dining room. Frances hung back, and remained behind until she and Miriam were alone on the porch.

"Are you happy for me?" she asked her sister diffidently.

"Of course," snapped Miriam. "Though why Billy would consent to stay in this house with Elinor is a thing I will never understand."

"Billy loves Mama!"

"Then he's a fool," said Miriam with a decisive nod. She peered at her sister, Frances, whose looks were suddenly downcast. "But if he loves you," said Miriam, softening, "then it doesn't matter one little bit whether he's a fool or not."

Frances looked up with a smile.

"Everything's gone be cold if we don't go down," said Miriam, and marched toward the door. As the sisters were going down the stairs, Miriam turned and spoke over her shoulder. "I don't know why you two didn't do what everybody else in this family has always done—just run off and get married. You better tell me right away what you want for a wedding present, 'cause I tell you, I am so busy at the mill I'm not gone have *any* time to go out shopping for it."

CHAPTER 52

Lake Pinchona

During the war, Queenie was taken care of by the Caskeys more than ever. She didn't have a job, and wanted no position but that of companion to James. James supplied her with money. Sister and Elinor gave her ration coupons. She never cooked because the Caskey tables were always open to her and to Lucille. Queenie was a bit of a poor relation, and she made herself useful in the ways that poor relations had always employed themselves: as fill-in companion, as runner of small errands, as listening post, and sometimes even as whipping boy. She had become, since the death of her husband, Carl, a clear-sighted woman who didn't bemoan her inferior circumstances. She did not resent the kindnesses that were done her, and she ignored the unconscious slights she occasionally perceived in the behavior of the Caskeys toward her and her children.

Queenie might have demanded more, had it not been for the problem of her offspring. Danjo belonged completely to James Caskey. No one would have interfered if she had claimed her rights as the boy's mother, except for the fact that Carl had fairly traded Danjo to James in exchange for a new automobile. This had been almost fifteen years before, but Queenie still had that car, though it now sat in her driveway, empty of gas. In commerce with James's house, Queenie saw her son frequently, but there was no more real parental love between them than there was between Elinor and Miriam. Queenie was like a distant aunt to Danjo. Sometimes Queenie sighed over this, not because she missed Danjo or regretted the bargain, but only because, of the three children she had borne, Danjo had turned out best. She often wished that either Malcolm or Lucille instead of Danjo had been the object of Carl and James's transaction.

Of her eldest, she heard little. Malcolm had trained at Camp Blanding, had been stationed at Fort Dix in New Jersey, and had reenlisted and been transferred to somewhere in Texas. He had been promoted twice and liked army life. Everybody who had known Malcom said blandly to Queenie, "The discipline will probably do that boy a lot of good. It's probably just what he really needed." Such criticism stung. Queenie suspected she had not been cut out for motherhood. Where her son spent his furloughs Queenie had no idea. She wondered whether she would ever see him again. With all the fighting in Europe and the Pacific, it seemed inevitable that Malcolm would soon be sent over. He wrote infrequently, and Queenie read every brief letter carefully, always with the thought in her head that it might prove to be his last communication.

Lucille was turning out no better than Malcolm. Behind the candy counter at the Ben Franklin, Lucille flirted with every soldier who walked into the store. She had also taken an evening job, waiting on tables out at Lake Pinchona. Queenie had not been in favor of this, but she could not refuse the girl the opportunity to make some extra money.

Lucille had a stack of photographs of Air Corps men tied with a yellow string in the top drawer of her dresser. Queenie had found it one day while searching for a button. On the weekend, Lucille spent all day and all evening out at the lake, where there were at least three military men for every local girl. Only once did Queenie venture to remonstrate, saying, "Darling, these aren't Perdido boys who are coming in from Eglin."

"Mama," said Lucille in her peeved, whining voice, "is that supposed to convey some meaning to me?"

"It just means that they didn't grow up with you. They don't know how sweet and innocent most Perdido girls are, and sometime one of them might try to go too far."

Lucille eyed her mother suspiciously. "Nobody's gone go too far with me, Ma. I don't even know why you'd want to say something like that to me. I'm just embarrassed to hear it spoke!"

Queenie said no more. In her unhappy heart, she knew for a certainty that her daughter *had* gone too far with one of the men from Eglin.

Lake Pinchona was a seven-mile drive from Perdido. The fifty-acre lake was irregular in shape, with many narrow fingers of forested land jutting out into the water and many secluded tongues of water lapping into the surrounding forest of pine, cedar, and cypress. On the western side of the lake was a pasture with a herd of Holstein cows. The grass on which those cows grazed was the thickest, greenest grass anyone in Perdido had ever seen. The colors of that grass, the water of the lake, and the skies that arched over the whole scene were like the colors in a paint box, mysterious and impossibly rich. The water of the lake was bright blue, and its fringes were thick with water lilies. Brave men unafraid of the alligators in the lake took their nervous girlfriends for rides in small boats. The alligators were so well fed by children dropping bread out of the windows of the dance hall, however, that there was little danger to those who ventured out onto the water.

Built next to a large picnic area beneath a grove of immense cedars, the dance hall was large, rectangular, and constructed entirely out over the water, with a gangway providing access from the land. A kitchen and a small screened-in dining room ran along one side, but most of the space was the dance area itself. It had a dark wooden floor, a shadowy vaulted ceiling, and a bench running around three sides beneath an uninterrupted line of windows. The place always seemed dim, not only because of the dark wood but because of the contrast of the bright light coming in through the windows and the front door. Outside, on the other side of the picnic area, were a concession stand, two small bathhouses, and a large swimming pool.

The lake was immensely popular during the war. It was close enough to Eglin to make returning to the base late at night no great difficulty. It attracted girls from Perdido, Bay Minette, Brewton, Atmore, Fairhope, Vaughn, Daphne, and even Mobile. Dancing began at five o'clock and ended at midnight. On weekends a band was hired, and a dollar admission fee charged. The place was run by a middle-aged couple, but they were so busy in the kitchen with hamburgers and hot dogs that they had little time to spend supervising those who came to the lake. Prudish folk in the surrounding towns began to whisper about what went on at Lake Pinchona, but the more sophisticated held that the dance floor of Lake Pinchona was a better place for the daughters of

Baldwin and Escambia counties than the back seat of an automobile.

Lucille waited tables—often quite ineptly—in the small dining room off the dance floor from six until nine every evening. She was the only waitress, and she sometimes gathered as much as four or five dollars in tips from the servicemen. When her shift was over, she hurried out to the darkened bathhouse and changed from her white uniform into a more becoming dress. Her favorite moment of the entire day was her reentrance into the dance hall, the hairnet and the shapeless white dress and apron of her waitress's uniform cast aside; her face was scrubbed, her hair brushed, her dress freshly pressed and still smelling of the sun it had been dried in that morning. All the Air Corps men flocked around her and said things like, "Are you sure you're the same girl who dropped the French fries and poured that coffee in my lap?" Lucille always laughed gaily, and returned, "That sure wasn't me, that was my twin sister!"

She danced with anyone who asked her. With the one she liked best during the course of the evening, she would sit pertly on the bench that ran around the room. She and that serviceman would turn and gaze out the windows at the moon and the stars and the shimmering water of the lake, with its ring of water lilies whitely glowing on their black pads. The dance hall was noisy and bright, but Lucille and the Air Corps man, feeling themselves more part of the dark, quiet night, would turn and look at each other and smile. At this juncture, Lucille would invariably ask in her coyest voice, "What's your name?"

Month succeeded month at Lake Pinchona, but Lucille never grew weary of her evening ritual. Her mother didn't see how she could keep it up: all day on her feet behind the candy counter at the Ben Franklin, waiting tables in the early evening, and then dancing until eleven or twelve. But Lucille didn't feel fatigue. "It's my war effort," she said airily.

An abnormally mild winter was followed by an unusually warm spring, and the lake opened for business several weeks early. Now the crowds were even heavier than the year before, and the kitchen hours were lengthened from six until ten. Lucille was still the only girl on the floor, but there weren't any more dropped plates of French fries or spilled cups of coffee. Her work was all done by rote. Her actions as much as her smile were distant and absent from her thoughts. Every minute she looked forward to that magic moment when she reentered the dance hall, transformed. She played over in her mind what compliments she had received in the past, and hoped that tonight one of the servicemen would say something she had never heard before. She glanced over the crowd, and wondered which one she would choose for her special partner tonight. She never decided beforehand and left the question to fate. Somehow the idea had caught in Lucille's head that every night's crowd at Lake Pinchona was different from that of the previous evening or the crowd of a week ago. She maintained this belief even though she remembered many faces from previous times. She held to this transparent fiction because she liked to imagine that her reappearance every night induced unparalleled wonder in the military men who witnessed her metamorphosis.

Elinor once spoke in confidence to Billy Bronze, saying, "Queenie is worried about Lucille, and just between you and me, Billy, she has reason to be. If you wouldn't mind, I wish you would take Frances—and Miriam if she wants to go—out to the lake once in a while and just keep an eye on Lucille. She's going to do pretty much whatever she wants to, I know that. But it would make Queenie feel better to have somebody watching out for her a little bit."

Thus, Billy and Frances, and even sometimes Miriam, went out to Lake Pinchona in the evening and danced. They waved to Lucille when they came in, ordered Cokes from her, smiled when she made her by now famous reentrance, and reminded her that Queenie worried when she stayed out after midnight.

Frances and Billy, without Miriam, were at the dance hall at Lake Pinchona one Saturday night shortly after their engagement. They had eaten supper with Elinor and Oscar, and afterward they had driven out to the lake. They walked hand in hand together beneath the cedars, then stood at the edge of the lake and stared at the dark water beneath the wide lily pads. On every side of them cicadas, chanting in unison, made it seem that every tree and bush sang.

At ten o'clock they went into the dance hall. The kitchen was just closing, so that the rattle of the dishes and talk of diners shouldn't intrude upon the dancers during the later, more intimate hours of the evening.

They stepped into the screened-in dining room just as Lucille was ushering the last reluctant customer out and latching the door behind him. It had been a busy evening, and Lucille looked frazzled and distracted. "I've got weary bones," she confided to Frances.

"Then maybe you should just go straight on home," suggested Frances.

Lucille stared at her cousin in disbelief. "It's Saturday night!" she cried, as if that explained everything.

Frances and Billy wandered off to speak to a couple of men from Eglin with whom they were acquainted. As undistracted and private in the empty

131

dining room as a fish in its aquarium, Lucille wiped the tables clean, set up for the following evening, counted her tips, and as she was taking off her apron, winked at the black dishwasher. She made a little show of going out through the kitchen door, saying loud good-nights to the owner's wife, who was wiping off the stove, and to the owner himself, who was taking admissions at the door. She skipped out into the night, her shoes beating a brief hollow tattoo on the wooden gangway.

Everyone in the dance hall knew that Lucille would return within a quarter hour. If Lucille had not been as pretty as she was, the little burletta played out nightly would have seemed ridiculous. The band continued to play, but fewer people danced. All the men wanted to see Lucille's entrance. The girls whispered among themselves that the reason Lucille worked at all, when she had such rich relatives, was so that she could buy those tacky little dresses that she put on in the bathhouse every night.

This night, however, they watched in vain, because Lucille did not return.

After a half hour of waiting, Frances became nervous. She went to the owner, and said, "Where is Lucille? I didn't think she usually took this long."

The owner only replied, "She's changing down at the bathhouse. I give her a key, 'cause nobody is allowed in there at night."

"Maybe she went home," said the owner's wife as she came out of the kitchen, wiping her hands on her dirty apron.

"Nope," said the owner. "I'd stake my life."

Frances signaled to Billy to remain and headed out the door. Her footsteps on the gangway over the edge of the lake echoed woodenly. The moon shone that night, but nothing of its light reached through the dense canopy of cedar branches. Frances pushed open the door of the bathhouse and called Lucille's name. Only a high-pitched, stertorous breathing came in reply.

She reached above her head and pulled the chain on the metal-shaded light that hung down from the ceiling. In its harsh illumination she saw Lucille lying twisted on the rough, puddled floor of the bathhouse. Her dress had been torn and raised up over her breasts. Her underpants had been pulled down to her ankles. Her lower belly and the inside of her thighs were bloody.

Lucille's eyes struggled to open. "Frances?" she whispered, as Frances began to pull Lucille's clothes back more or less into place.

"Oh, Lord. Oh, Lord!" Frances whispered. "Let's get you home."

"Travis Gann," said Lucille, struggling to rise. "It was Travis Gann."

"I thought he was still in jail!"

Lucille shook her head. With that motion, she lost her fragile balance, and her head dropped back against the rough wooden floor with a loud knock.

"You lie there. I'll get Billy," said Frances.

Lucille made no reply; her breathing was rough.

Frances rose, knocking her head against the light, so that it danced and threw violent shadows and shafts of light over the interior of the women's bathhouse. Frances backed out the door—unaccountably knocking her head again, this time on the top of the doorframe.

Everything was different for Frances as she left the bathhouse with the intention of returning to the dance hall and fetching Billy. For one thing, it no longer seemed night. Before, she had had to almost feel her way along the path to the bathhouse with her arms outstretched, the night dark beneath the canopy of cedar boughs. Now, on her way back, she saw as easily as she might have seen at high noon, when the sun glanced blindingly off the surface of Lake Pinchona.

She had wanted to run to bring Billy out, but something was different about her legs, that didn't allow running. She loped and swayed, and her head was thrust forward.

Everything *looked* different too: her vision was blurred, and she saw things from a different height. The ground seemed farther away.

Even as these differences registered in Frances's mind, that mind itself changed. Frances Caskey no longer had thoughts that belonged to Lucille's cousin.

Her hearing was acute. To her right, among a grove of cypresses on a little tongue of spongy land, she heard a footstep on the soft ground. Without any conscious thought, the thing that was no longer Frances Caskey turned in that direction.

At the same time, that thing caught another sound, this one much louder, an echoing footfall on the gangway from the dance hall. She—for though she was no longer Frances, she was yet *female*—slipped into the darkness, and avoided Billy on his way out to the bathhouse.

She slipped among the trees and was hidden in the darkness, her progress marked by a series of wet slaps against the cypress and cedar trunks. She heard more footfalls, then a curse word that conveyed no meaning to her altered mind, but did serve to pinpoint the location of its speaker.

She saw him long before he saw her. His form appeared vague and indistinct, but brightly lighted, as if she had gazed at him on a sunlit beach through squinted eyes.

Travis Gann, standing near the shore of the lake, had turned at the unfamiliar, moist slapping noise. In the darkness, beneath the trees, he saw, indistinctly, pale, nonhuman staring eyes, a wide flat gleaming face, an enormous lipless mouth, a tall, strong form to which the tattered remnants of a girl's dress clung wetly. Vast webbed feet flapped against the ground as it came nearer. He backed against a tree and pressed as if he might push it down behind him. The tree did not fall, and Travis Gann sidled around it to the right. He lost his footing on the slippery ground and slid with a splash among the lily pads at the lake's edge. A large moth flew against his face, and he saw the frantic beating of its white, dusty wings. The mud of the lake was soft, and when he tried to stand, his feet sank deep. When he tried to scramble away, tearing at the lilies, he discovered that he was caught in the twisted underwater stems of the plants. He looked up, and the thing that had appeared to him amongst the trees a few moments before, now stood above him in the moonlight. He saw it for only one moment of stark terror, for it slipped down the bank and into the water beside him.

Moving beneath the water, Frances's vision cleared. Everything was as bright as before. The lilies were a waving forest of thin brown trunks, and among them she saw the man struggling, one foot caught in the mud. She surged toward him, thrust out one arm to catch him, and in the same easy motion, pushed off toward the center of the lake.

Travis's head remained above water as he was suddenly pulled backward, free of the lilies, into the open black water of Lake Pinchona. With a fearful jerk, he remembered the alligators. Then, for an instant, he grinned. Why should he fear alligators when *this* thing had caught hold of him? The grin faded, and Travis Gann stared up at the sky. The stars raced along above him. He heard the water rushing past his ears and water poured chokingly into his open mouth.

The thing that was Frances Caskey swam out to the middle of the lake, and when it had got there it swung its other arm around Travis Gann. Holding him close, she plunged down to the muddy bottom. She held him in her embrace as a father might hold an overgrown boy on his lap. She gazed into his face as a father might have gazed.

So deep were they beneath the water that Travis could see nothing but the pale luminescence of the two eyes that stared at him. He struggled and squirmed, but was held fast. The little air remaining in his lungs was exhaled in a stifled shout. He freed one arm, made a fist, and jammed it against the wide, flat face in front of him. His fist met nothing at all. His mind registered bewilderment, and his last conscious thought was the solution to that mystery: *It opened its mouth, and my fist went right in.* Then the mouth clamped shut over Travis Gann's forearm, and the entire arm was wrenched from its socket.

Travis Gann knew nothing after that.

Frances ate both Travis's arms. Sometime in the course of that feeding, Travis Gann died. When her hunger was sated, Frances carried the corpse over to the alligator nest she knew lay at the edge of the cow pasture. Attracted by the smell of blood in the water, the alligators were there to receive him.

Frances stood up out of the water, holding aloft the armless corpse. Blood spilled from the empty sockets. Her own bloody mouth opened and she piped a series of brief shrill notes. The water all around was agitated by the thrashing tails of the alligators—and her own. Somewhere, in a dark corner of the creature's mind, Frances Caskey was startled to hear the shrill piping song that she remembered from her dreams.

Frances Caskey sang, and Travis Gann was tumbled into the alligators' nest on the banks of Lake Pinchona.

CHAPTER 53

Mother and Daughter

When Billy reached the bathhouse, he found Lucille as Frances had left her only minutes before. He gathered Lucille up into his arms and hurried along the cedar path with her, pausing once behind a tree to allow a knot of soldiers to pass. He slipped out to the parking lot, laid Lucille across the back seat of the car, and covered her with a blanket from the trunk. Returning to the dance hall with as much nonchalance as he could muster, he reassured the owner and his wife that all was well. Lucille had merely fallen prey to an upset stomach, and he was taking her home. He stood just outside the door of the dance hall, causing the gangway to creak beneath his weight as he shifted back and forth in confusion and nervousness. The yellow light from within spilled out in discrete squares all around the building, but did not dispel the darkness. The moon was now obscured by clouds.

Billy could easily imagine that Frances had fled

in silent hysteria when she found her cousin in that horrifying condition in the bathhouse. He went back to the car, hoping Frances would be there. She was not. Lucille moaned softly. Billy got into the car, unsure as to what he should do. Lucille might require medical attention, but he did not want to leave without Frances. He got out of the car, cautioning an unheedful Lucille of the necessity of remaining quiet.

Billy returned to the bathhouse and softly called Frances's name. When there was no reply, he decided to search further. Keeping clear of the dance hall, he entered the grove of cedar and cypress at the edge of the lake. The music from the dance hall was frequently drowned out by the noise of the cicadas anchored in the bark of the trees. He went to the edge of the water. The moon came out from behind a cloud, and shone upon the lake.

"Frances?" he called.

A head broke the surface of the water about fifty feet from shore. It wasn't Frances—it wasn't even human. It disappeared so quickly that Billy told himself that he'd imagined it—even though he was certain he hadn't. While he was telling himself, *it was just an alligator,* he noticed a trail forming itself in ripples on the surface of the calm black water of the lake. The trail came toward him. He backed away into the darkness and security of the trees.

It saw me.

Frances rose among the lily pads and weakly called Billy's name.

He rushed forward, and pulled his fiancée up onto the land. She had lost her shoes and her feet were covered with mud. Her dress and underclothes hung from her in shreds. Billy took off his jacket and draped it over her shoulders.

"Shhh!" he said, when she looked as though she was about to speak. "Let's just get back to the car."

On the way home, Frances was silent. She did not

explain how she had come to be in the lake, or why so little was left of her dress. Billy did not press the matter. He pulled up in front of Elinor's house, got out and hurried inside, cautioning Frances and Lucille to remain in the car. He brought out Elinor and Zaddie with blankets, and the two young women were soon installed in the bedrooms upstairs. Queenie was telephoned and arrived in a few minutes.

Travis Gann, Lucille said, had raped her. He had been waiting for her just outside the bathhouse. He had grabbed her by the shoulders, pushed her inside, knocked her to the floor, pulled up her dress, ripped off her pants, and punctured her hymen in his first thrust.

Queenie's eyebrows were raised—she had not imagined that the thing had been intact. It was only then so much the worse for her poor daughter.

Frances would see no one but her mother. Elinor took Frances into the bathroom and kneeled beside the bathtub to bathe her daughter tenderly. In a low, distant voice, Frances told her mother all she remembered about her experience at the lake.

"Mama, I killed him."

"He was a terrible man," said Elinor reassuringly. "He raped Lucille. He got Malcolm in trouble."

"But I *killed* him."

"Nobody knows that, darling, except you and me. And even if anybody knew, do you think they'd do anything but give you a medal?" Elinor gave a low laugh. "What do you think Queenie would say? Queenie would say, 'Frances, I've got to kiss you for killing that old Travis Gann, now we're not ever going to have to see his ugly face again.' Stand up, darling."

Frances stood obediently, as of old, with her feet a little apart. Her mother began to rub her belly with a soapy cloth.

139

"You know what, Mama?" said Frances, when Elinor had begun washing her right leg.

"What?"

"It's not even so much the business about killing Travis Gann..."

"What is it, then?"

"It's *how* I did it."

"What do you mean *how?*"

"How?" repeated Frances. "I dragged him down to the bottom of the lake. And I bit off his arms. I got his arms *inside my mouth* and I bit them off. I ate both his arms."

Elinor said, "Give me your foot, baby."

Frances obediently raised her leg and placed it on the edge of the bathtub for her mother to wash.

Mechanically, when this was done, Frances turned around, and her mother began on her left leg.

"What's wrong, darling?" asked Elinor after a bit. "What are you thinking of?"

"I'm trying to remember if that was exactly what happened. It couldn't have happened that way really, could it? Already it seems like a dream."

"It was a bad dream," returned her mother. "Now turn this way, face me." Frances did so. Her mother stood, looked at Frances, and held her gaze. Elinor took her daughter's arm in her right hand, and with the other she began to wash between Frances's legs. "Do you know what really happened out at the lake?" Frances shook her head. "You found Lucille," said Elinor slowly, and went on with deliberateness, "and then you ran to get Billy so that he could help get her out of there. But Travis Gann was lying in wait for you, and he attacked you and tore off your clothes and when you tried to run away from him you fell in the water. You couldn't see because it was so dark. Travis came in after you, but he couldn't swim as well as you could and the alligators came and got him."

Frances's gaze, which had turned glassy, hardened into focus. "Yes, ma'am," she said quietly.

Elinor sighed, dropped the washcloth, and embraced her naked daughter. "I'm so sorry, darling. I'm so sorry it had to happen *this* way!"

Frances was stiff in her arms. When Elinor let go, Frances said, "It *did* happen, though, what I really remember."

Elinor nodded.

"Stand out of the bathtub, darling, and let me dry you off."

Frances did so. She said, "It was horrible, Mama."

Elinor, who had taken a fresh towel from the rack, looked at Frances in surprise. "No, it wasn't," she said. "You just say that now. But were you hurt? Were you frightened? Were you ever in danger?"

"I don't remember..."

Elinor shook her head. "You weren't, darling, not for one minute." She placed the towel around Frances's shoulders and began to rub. "That old Travis Gann could never have hurt you, not when you were..."

"Were what?"

"Were the way you were when you got out in the water."

"It didn't happen in the water, Mama. It happened in the bathhouse, right after I found Lucille."

Elinor nodded. She dropped to her knees again and continued to towel Frances dry. "That's because you were upset. You were upset on Lucille's account. I don't blame you, either. Not one little bit."

"Mama, is this ever gone happen again?"

Elinor didn't answer. She stood up, tossed the towel into the corner of the bathroom, and took a robe from a hook on the door. "Put this on. Let's go in the other room and let me brush your hair."

"Mama," said Frances calmly, as she allowed herself to be lead into the next room, "you got to tell me

141

this time. You cain't keep on putting me off and putting me off when I ask you about things. Not after what happened tonight. *I killed somebody,*" she whispered.

Oscar and Billy were sitting on the screened-in porch, onto which opened the window of Frances's room. Oscar, when he saw the light come on, came over to the window and peered in. "Elinor," he said, "is she all right?"

"She's fine," returned Elinor, guiding her daughter to the vanity. Frances sat woodenly on the wicker seat before the triptych mirror.

"What the hell happened out there?"

"Travis Gann," said Elinor.

"Are we gone have to call the police?"

"No!" said Elinor sharply. "Oscar, will you just let Frances and me alone for a while? I will come out there a little later and tell everybody what happened and explain what we're going to do. Don't you trust me?"

Oscar shrugged. "Billy and me are sitting here on our hands and we just don't know *what* to do next."

"Fine," said Elinor, "you just continue with that." Despite the heat of the evening, Elinor pulled down the window in her husband's face and snapped the curtains shut. She returned to her daughter. Frances sat with her hands in her lap, blankly staring at her triple reflection in the mirrors. Elinor picked up a brush and began pulling it through the thick ropes of her daughter's damp hair.

"Frances," said Elinor quietly, smiling down at her daughter's reflection as she brushed, "what you've got to do is calm down, because in just a little while you and I are going to have to go out on the porch and talk to Oscar and Billy and Queenie. You're going to have to tell them what happened out at the lake. They're going to expect you to be a little upset, but they're not going to want to listen to any wild stories."

"Mama," sighed Frances, looking neither at herself nor at her mother, but staring instead at the little lamp with the fringed shade, "you don't think I'd go to *anybody* with a story like that, do you?"

"I hope not. Who'd believe you? Nobody would. *I* wouldn't even believe you." Elinor gave a little laugh.

"Mama, it's not funny."

"Frances, darling, you act like this has never happened before—that's what I can't understand."

Frances looked up at her mother's reflection in astonishment.

After a few moments, Elinor said quietly, "I see what it is. You don't remember..."

"Don't remember?"

"The other times."

"*What* other times, Mama?"

"The other times when you went out in the water."

"You mean," said Frances hesitantly, "I had that *change*...?"

Elinor nodded. "Of course. When you used to go down to the Gulf with Miriam, and you'd swim and swim for hours and hours—you don't think a sixteen-year-old girl could swim out that far, do you? A sixteen-year-old girl who had spent three years of her life in that bed right over there, not even able to move her legs when she wanted to? You remember when you were little and you and I used to go swimming in the Perdido together, and we wouldn't let anybody else go with us? Remember that?"

"A little," admitted Frances. "I don't remember that anything happened, though, I just remember..."

"What?"

"Nothing, Mama. That's just it, I can't remember anything about it. Just that everything was different."

Elinor nodded sagely.

"That's it, then," said Frances mournfully. "When I'm in the water, and I can't remember things, that's what happens to me?"

"That's right."

"But tonight I remembered more."

Elinor shrugged. "More things happened, and you were upset. And also you're getting older."

"Then this *is* all gone happen again?"

Elinor only went on with her brushing. She didn't answer.

After a moment, Frances said delicately, "Mama?"

"Yes?"

"Mama, not everybody is like this..."

"No, darling, just you and me."

"Not Miriam?"

Elinor shook her head. "Remember when I said that *you* were my real little girl? That's what I meant."

Frances sat very still and stared at her visage in the mirror. She raised her arm and turned it in the light, inspecting it.

"You won't see anything, darling," said Elinor.

"What about Billy?"

"What about him?" asked Elinor. She put aside the brush and opened a little gilt box with bobby pins inside. She pulled back a thick wave of Frances's hair and reached for a pin. Frances held the wave in place until her mother had secured it.

"Can I still marry him?"

"Of course! I married your father, didn't I?"

Frances shrugged. "What do I tell him?"

"Don't tell him anything!" cried Elinor. "What do you imagine you would say to him?"

"I don't know!" exclaimed Frances helplessly. She spun around on the wicker seat and looked at her mother directly. "Mama, I don't understand *any* of this, and you've got to help me! You've got to tell me what to do!"

Elinor took Frances's shoulders, squeezed them, and said, "You're doing everything just right. If you have any problems, you come to me. That's all. Now turn around and let me finish doing your hair. They're waiting for us!"

"Why fix it at all?"

"Because when we go out on the porch, and you see Billy again, I don't want him to remember anything of what you looked like out at the lake. I just want him to see my pretty, pretty little girl."

"Mama, does Daddy know?"

"Know about what?"

"About me?"

"No."

"About you?"

Elinor paused. "Oscar knows more than he's willing to say. Your daddy is a good man, darling, and he's very smart. Your daddy knows when to be quiet. Billy is just like him, don't you think?"

Frances didn't answer. Another question already occupied her mind.

"What about children?"

"What about them?" asked Elinor, looking this way and that at Frances's reflection, checking her hair.

"Will they be like us?"

Elinor smiled. "You're all done," she said, "and you've asked enough questions for one evening. Let's go out on the porch and get this business over with."

CHAPTER 54

Lucille and Grace

Lucille stayed in bed a week after her rape, nursed by all the Caskey women. Townfolk were told that at Lake Pinchona, in the dark, Lucille had tripped over the root of a cedar tree, fallen, and cut herself on a nail sticking out of a post.

The owner of the recreation facilities at Lake Pinchona and his wife had their suspicions, of course, but they had no interest in spreading news of a rape. If it had become known that a local girl had been attacked by an Air Corps man—it was *bound* to have been a soldier, since for the past year it was mostly soldiers who had come to the lake—there would have been hell to pay. The lake might have been put off limits by the commander at Eglin, and where would the couple's comfortable profits have gone?

Another waitress was hired, a girl from Bay Minette who wasn't nearly so pretty as Lucille and had never learned to dance. After she had recovered from her "fall," Lucille wasn't at all interested in returning to her former position.

No trace of Travis Gann ever turned up in the lake or on its shores. Perdido assumed that Travis, in the due course of justice, had been released from Atmore prison and had simply disappeared. Perdido was glad that he had taken up residence someplace far away.

A couple of months later, Queenie found that the full force of her old bad luck had come upon her again. Lucille was pregnant. On Elinor's advice, Lucille had been examined not by Dr. Benquith next door but rather by a man in Pensacola. The Caskeys hadn't wanted their friend Leo to know what had occurred out at Lake Pinchona. "I know pregnancy when I see it," said Queenie. "In another couple of months she'll start to show."

One evening at James's there was a conference of the Caskey women, with only Frances and Miriam excused. Lucille was brought over to the house, but relegated to Grace's bedroom with the door closed. The question "What do we do?" was what the women had gathered to decide.

Grace looked around with pleasure. This was her first major family conference; she was proud to have been admitted to it. Here she might give her maiden speech, and she wanted the family to remember it. "Let me take her away," said Grace.

"Take her where?" said Sister.

"It doesn't matter. Miami, maybe, or Tennessee. It doesn't really matter where. Tell people she's visiting relatives, or she's keeping me company on a tour of the national parks, something like that."

"You can't travel around much," Elinor pointed out, "remember there's a war going on."

"Then we'll sit in one place," said Grace. "A place where nobody knows us."

"For nine months?" said Queenie. "You'd stay with Lucille for nine months?"

"It wouldn't be nine, it'd be more like seven."

"What would you do with the baby when it's born?" asked Sister.

Grace shrugged. "I don't know. She cain't keep it, I guess. Then there'd be no reason to go away and keep it a secret. Put it up for adoption, I suppose."

"I wish we could keep it..." sighed Queenie. "Maybe we could give it to James."

"James is too old," said Elinor, not unkindly, "to care for a baby. And if we were to keep it, everybody would know where it came from. We'll have to give it away."

Grace soon understood that they had accepted the wisdom of her proposal and that she would take Lucille away for the duration of the pregnancy. She said then, "We can decide about the baby later. First we have to decide how Lucille and I are gone get out of town without anybody suspecting anything. See, first she's gone have to quit that job at the Ben Franklin..."

It was arranged that evening. Lucille was informed and acquiesced in everything. She was a changed girl since the rape; not dour, but distracted. She no longer lied because there didn't seem to be anything in life worth lying for. She no longer whined to get her way. She looked at Grace and said, "Are you gone take care of me?"

"Yes," said Grace. "Where had you rather go, Nashville or Miami?"

Lucille shrugged.

"Nashville, then," said Grace. "We can tell everybody we're visiting your relatives, Queenie."

"They're all dead," said Queenie.

"All the better," said Grace. "Then we won't be disturbed."

* * *

149

Perdido heard only that Grace and Lucille, who had never been close before, were going off to Nashville for an indefinite stay. There was something mysterious in this, if only because it seemed so unlikely that Grace would leave her father completely alone in Perdido, when James was still grieving in the wake of Danjo's absence. Perdido learned nothing except that questions were unwelcome.

James demanded a single alteration in the plan. He would not hear of his daughter going so far away as Nashville. He wanted Grace and Lucille hidden away a little closer to home. Oscar, thinking the matter over, said, "You know what? Right after Mama died and we bought all that land over in Escambia County—y'all remember? Elinor had me buy up a little piece of property that had been foreclosed on. It's maybe five, ten miles south of Babylon, off this little road that doesn't go anywhere at all. You never saw anyplace so far away from anything in your life. Elinor, you and I drove over there one day, remember?"

Elinor remembered it well. "The place is called Gavin Pond," she said. "There's an old farmhouse next to a fishing pond. Plenty of artesian water around there. It's got a pasture and a pecan orchard, and five, six hundred acres of decent timber. The Perdido River is the western boundary of the property."

"Y'all never even mentioned this place before," said James.

Oscar said, "After Mama died and left us her money, Elinor and I were buying up property right and left. Well, it looks like it might come in handy now. Gavin Pond—I'd even forgot the name of it."

"How long does it take to get there from here?" asked Grace.

"Half an hour, maybe," said Elinor. "Take the road over to Babylon, and then south, that's all."

"Daddy," said Grace, "you and Queenie would be able to come see us all the time. Elinor, what shape was that old farmhouse in last time you were there?"

"It was all right," said Elinor. "But by now it could probably use some work. I'll drive over tomorrow, and take Bray along and see what all needs to be done before you can move in."

Elinor and Bray began work the next day. In the following week, Bray killed a family of squirrels in the second-floor bedrooms and repaired a hole in the roof. He put new steps on the back, and shored up the narrow front porch. Meanwhile, early every morning, before the rest of Perdido was awake, Elinor and Sister tied furniture to the back of a small mill truck and had Bray drive it out to the place. It had been decided that the purchase of new furniture—either in Perdido or Babylon—would have excited too much local curiosity. Queenie went to the Crawford's store, filled her car with groceries, and stocked the kitchen. The Caskeys visited the house by ones and twos and nobody in Perdido learned anything of it, or suspected the Caskeys' scheme. Lucille quit her job at the Ben Franklin, and was not sorry to do so. She no longer had any interest in flirting with the servicemen who wandered in for a bag of peanut clusters or a Mounds bar.

In the middle of August, when the house was finally judged ready, Queenie drove her daughter down to Pensacola to a beauty parlor. Lucille's hair was cut short and then dyed black. They came back to Perdido only after night had fallen. From there Lucille and Grace drove off with half a dozen suitcases in the back seat. The Caskeys remained inside their houses as the car pulled away from James's house, and Lucille crouched low in the seat as they drove through downtown Perdido, crossed the bridge over the river, and went through Baptist Bottom on the road that led eastward to Florida. Lucille wept.

Babylon in 1943 was a tiny place, smaller than Perdido, without a mill or any other major business to make it profitable, and nothing to distinguish it but the three young men who in the past three years had all gone on to play professional baseball. The Caskey property lay five miles south of town, out a gravel road through the colored section. Two pebbly ruts led away from that road through a hardwood forest; half a mile farther along this track they came to the clearing with the farmhouse in it. Behind the farmhouse was the cattle pasture, where only deer had grazed for twenty years, and the pecan orchard with a little stream running through it. The orderly rows had been disturbed by oak saplings growing up anarchically in their midst. Beside the house was the fishing pond, filled with fish that had fed and grown and multiplied for undisturbed generations. The pond was bordered by dark, moss-hung cypresses. All this, of course, was not apparent in the deep night of Grace and Lucille's arrival. They saw only the ruts of the track, the trunks of trees, and the lowest clapboards of the house in the wavering lights of the headlamps.

The modest house had two rooms up and two rooms down, with a pantry and bath on the first floor. Elinor had run up curtains for the windows. The floors were hardwood, and Zaddie and Luvadia had scrubbed them. None of this operation had been kept secret from the Sapps. They would have found out anyway, and the Caskeys considered them all family, trusting them as they trusted themselves. But despite all these small attempts to make the place seem comfortable and familiar, Lucille thought she had never been in a place so removed and lonely in her life. All the windows looked out on blackness.

Lucille clung to Grace. "I'm scared."

"We'll go upstairs," said Grace, "and I'll show you our bedrooms."

Lucille turned to Grace in terror. "I cain't sleep by myself. Not way out here!"

The bedrooms upstairs were square and unadorned, a bed, a dresser, a vanity, and a hooked rug in each. In the day they might be cheerful enough, with sunlight beating in through the high windows, but at night they were stuffy with the day's heat. The single overhead bulb in each room lighted the rooms poorly, casting harsh shadows, and picking out the dead flies that littered the windowsill and the wasps' nest in the corner of the ceiling of Grace's room.

"I hate it here," said Lucille.

"Tomorrow I'll take you fishing," said Grace. "We'll have the time of our lives."

Lucille shook her head doubtfully. Neither that night nor the nights that followed would Lucille permit Grace to sleep in her own room. She insisted that they share the same bed. Lucille was frightened of the dark and the overwhelming quiet outside. The silence was broken only by the occasional *plop* of a fish in the pond, or the crackle of breaking twigs as animals roamed through the forest. When she looked out she saw only the cold moon over Babylon reflected in the water of Gavin Pond. On the other side of the pond was a tiny graveyard with a dozen tombstones under which were buried all the members of the family who had built the farmhouse, and who had slept in the room she slept in now. No, Lucille wasn't sleeping by herself. All night long she cowered in Grace's arms, despite the heat and the closeness of the room. She was never certain in what her fear was centered, whether it was the quiet and the dark, or the pond and the graveyard and the moonlight—or whether it was the thing that was expanding inside her belly.

Things were better during the day. The house had cooled off somewhat during the night. The disposition of the trees kept sunlight off the roof until late afternoon, but then the place quickly heated up. Lucille listened to the radio and played records, sat in the boat and slapped at mosquitoes while Grace fished, wandered in the pecan orchard with a big stick poised to beat off snakes, and sometimes did a little sewing. "I keep wanting to do something for the baby," she confessed to Grace, "and then all of a sudden I remember I'm not gone keep him. I bet it *is* a him and not a her."

They weren't as lonely as Lucille had anticipated on the night of their arrival. The Caskeys came out to see them, sometimes James and Queenie, sometimes Elinor and Zaddie, sometimes Sister alone. The visitors sat in chairs placed out by the pond, and everyone would say how pleasant it was, and it was just a wonder they hadn't thought of fixing up this place before. It was *much* nicer than the beach. Twice Oscar drove out in the middle of the day, saying he had just had to get away from the mill; all that business was driving him crazy. Only Frances and Miriam did not come. Once, when they were out on the pond fishing, Lucille asked Grace why she thought her cousins stayed away. Grace at first didn't answer. Then after a few moments she said, "They think you and I are in Nashville."

"You mean everybody's keeping this a secret, even from them?"

"They're too young. They might let it out, without intending to," explained Grace.

For some reason, this depressed Lucille. She seemed to see in Frances and Miriam's ignorance of her plight the real extent of her shame. She cried, "It's not my fault! I didn't ask that man to jump on top of me in the bathhouse!"

154

Grace pulled a fish into the boat. She was about to give up the fishing—in such a pond as this, it was no sport at all. Besides, something in the water gave the fish a rancid taste, no matter how soon they were cooked, as if they had fed off only the dead fish that had sunk to the bottom. "Of course it's not your fault, Lucille. Who said it was your fault?"

"Then why am I being punished?"

"You call a vacation like this punishment?"

"I do, when I cain't even go into Babylon with you."

"How often do I go in? Once a week, maybe. Queenie brings us food. I don't even like to go in town."

"I feel like I'm in jail. Nobody asked me what *I* wanted to do about all this."

Grace looked up in surprise. "Did you want to keep this child? When you knew that its father was that no-good Travis Gann? Let's just hope Frances is right and those alligators out at Lake Pinchona *did* eat him up!"

Lucille looked away. "I don't know what I wanted to do. I wasn't thinking straight. I'm not thinking straight now."

"Pull down your hat," said Grace. "You're getting too much sun on your face."

"Why are we out here?" demanded Lucille suddenly. "Why cain't we let anybody know?"

"For one simple reason," returned Grace. "We don't want anybody to know what happened to you. And the reason for that is not 'cause *we're* ashamed, but because of what would happen to you if everybody did find out. Travis Gann jumping on top of you is not your fault, you're right, but if it comes out that he did it, and you got pregnant, everybody's gone look at you different. And they'd certainly treat that little baby different. I'd be surprised if you could ever get married after that. Perdido's mean about things

155

like that. People everywhere are, I guess. Men don't want to marry damaged goods, and that's what you'd be, if anybody found out. Damaged goods."

"I don't care!" cried Lucille. "I don't want to get married. Not ever."

Grace laughed. "Lucille Strickland! I have seen you flirt with every man who came within a three mile radius of that candy counter at the Ben Franklin. I have seen you try on your mama's wedding ring time and time again just to see what it looked like! Don't tell me you aren't interested in getting married."

"I'm not, though." She looked around, at the pond, at the graveyard, at the house, at the sky, as if in puzzlement that such a decision had been made in her mind without her having had a single thing to say in the matter. "I'm not, though," she repeated softly. "Maybe this place isn't so bad after all. It's just a little lonely out here, that's all."

"You sound just like Daddy," said Grace. "Y'all act like I wasn't even around to keep y'all company. I think I'm gone pick this fish up and wave it in your ungrateful face!"

As she did so, Lucille laughed and squealed, and cried, "No, don't do it! Please don't do it, Grace!"

CHAPTER 55

Tommy Lee Burgess

Three times Lucille was taken to see a doctor in Pensacola, and every time was assured that the pregnancy was proceeding in perfect order. The doctor predicted that the child would be healthy and—considering the size of Lucille's belly—large. Elinor and Sister had quietly expected that through impatience and loneliness Lucille would give up their careful charade and return to Perdido, pregnant and unmarried, leaving Queenie to bear up under the scandal. Queenie secretly expected that, too. Yet, as the family made its visits to Gavin Pond it became apparent that Lucille was settling in, that she was not the girl she had been, and that her life had altered in unforeseen ways. She was becoming content with her straitened lot in the remote farmhouse south of Babylon.

During that autumn Lucille did not chafe at her loneliness. She did not pine for the company of young Air Corps men, or for her female chums at the Ben

Franklin and Lake Pinchona. She seemed content to sit in the house all day, embroidering pillowcases and nightgowns while Grace explored the property she had come to feel was hers. Each thought the company of the other was sufficient. Queenie, Elinor, and Sister sometimes felt they were an intrusion on the cherished solitude of the cousins.

Who had ever known Lucille to do anything so painstaking and sedate and long-lasting as embroidery? Next, wonder of wonders, she took up dressmaking. She asked her mother once if they could afford a sewing machine. The next day James and Bray brought a Singer in one of the mill trucks. The Perdido visitors always brought Lucille lengths of fabric and a new dress pattern, in her size or in Grace's. Lucille was filling the closets of the farmhouse with homemade dresses.

Grace said she wished she had lived in the country all her life. When her birthday came up in January, James had asked his daughter what she wanted. Grace replied, "A tractor." He bought her one, and Grace set about restoring the pecan orchard to its former splendor. One afternoon in February, Bray drove James and Queenie out to Gavin Pond, and they sat in the living room of the farmhouse talking with their respective daughters. Grace had constructed her cousin an adjustable embroidery frame. In the advanced months of her pregnancy, Lucille had found it difficult to sit up for long periods of time. She lay on one of the sofas in the room, with the frame tilted at just the right angle over her extended belly, so that she could continue her work without strain. To Queenie and James's astonishment, Grace talked of the time—after the arrival of the baby—when she and Lucille would drive over to Georgia and buy a few head of cattle. Grace was certain that within a year she could turn Gavin

Pond—as the entire tract of land was, imprecisely, called—into a paying proposition.

"Grace," cried Queenie, "you mean you are thinking of *living* out here!"

"We love it here," said Grace. "And after all this work..."

"James," put in Lucille, "do you have an old rug you don't want? Something for this room? I was thinking..."

"Blue," said James. "It'd have to be blue."

"Wait a minute," said Queenie. "James, don't start putting rugs in here until we get all this straight."

"Get what straight, Mama?" Lucille asked.

"Do you *like* it here, darling?"

"Mama," said Lucille contentedly, slipping her needle into the fabric she was working on, "we just love it."

"Don't you miss the town?"

Lucille shook her head. "We've got the radio, and that's all there is to do in Perdido anyway. After the baby comes, Grace said she'd take me over to DeFuniak Springs to the movies any time we wanted to go. If I went back to Perdido I'd have to go back to work at the Ben Franklin. I've got lazy. I don't want to work. James, next time somebody comes out here, can you send that rug with them?"

"Lucille is dying for that rug, Daddy."

"What else would you like to have?" asked James. "I guess you want to fix this place up nice, don't you?"

This abrupt change in Lucille Strickland was only a two-hours' wonder in the Caskey family. No one thought it strange that Grace and Lucille should take up housekeeping together, and each be perfectly happy in the sole company of the other. It was only thought peculiar that they should want to keep house at Gavin Pond. No Caskey had ever lived in the country.

"My little girl," said James, "wants to be a farmer. More power to her."

"And my little girl," said Queenie, "wants to be a farmer's wife. Who would have thought it?"

"I guess," said Sister, "that when the baby comes, and they give it away, then we can just tell everybody that Grace has bought a farm out in the country and that Lucille is out there keeping her from getting lonesome."

"And everybody will think they're *both* out of their minds," sighed Elinor.

No one in the family dissuaded Grace and Lucille from their course. Every time someone went over to visit, he took some household object with him: a lamp, or small table, or a box of books. "First thing we are gone do is fix up the guest room," said Lucille once when her mother had come for a visit, "so that anytime any of you wants to stay overnight you can."

Queenie looked up, surprised, and said, "But there are only two bedrooms in this house, one for you and one for Grace. Where is the guest room?"

"Oh, Mama," laughed Lucille. "Grace and I sleep together! You don't think I'd sleep all by myself way out here in the country, do you? You know how scared I get."

The Caskeys absorbed this somewhat startling information too. Everyone remembered that as a child, Lucille had suffered from recurrent nightmares.

Perhaps with all these small surprises along the way, the Caskeys should have been prepared for the bombshell that appeared at the end, but they were not.

When the time approached for Lucille to give birth, Ivey Sapp came to stay at Gavin Pond, sleeping on a cot in the kitchen. To maintain secrecy regarding the pregnancy, no doctor was to be called in. Without complication, and in the bed she shared with Grace Caskey, Lucille Strickland delivered a perfect male baby, who weighed about as much as a five-pound sack of flour, according to Ivey's trustworthy estimate.

Queenie, James, Elinor, and Sister arrived an hour later, and looked at the child.

"We're calling him Thomas Lee," said Grace proudly, standing by Lucille at the head of the bed. "Hey there, Tommy Lee!"

"There is no point in naming the child," said Queenie. "You ought to let his new parents give him a name. They may already have a boy called Tommy."

"New parents?" cried Lucille. "Who said anything about new parents?" She held the infant protectively against her breast.

Queenie, James, Elinor, and Sister all stared at one another.

"You...mean," said Elinor slowly, "that you intend on... *keeping* this child?"

"He is a *pretty* boy!" said James. *"I'd* keep him."

"James," said Sister. "you would keep any child that came your way. I am surprised you haven't been taken up for kidnapping."

Elinor looked at the two young women. She sighed. "Let's get it straight, then," she said. "First of all, you want to stay out here in this godforsaken place..."

"Yes, ma'am," said Grace staunchly.

Lucille nodded diffidently.

"And you want to keep the baby."

"He's ours!" cried Lucille.

"Darling," said Queenie, "we're only thinking of what's best for you."

The four elder Caskeys, like a tribunal, glanced at one another once and then twice, looked at Grace, Lucille, and Tommy Lee, and glanced at one another again. As head of the family, Elinor spoke. "Of course you can keep the child, and of course you can stay on out here. You're both over twenty-one and you can both do whatever you want to do. We just want

161

you both to be happy: Now are you *sure* this is what is going to make you happy?"

"Yes," both answered as one voice.

"Then tell us," said Elinor, "what we're supposed to say in Perdido."

"What do you mean?" asked Grace.

"I am surprised," said Elinor, "that we have been able to keep all this secret for as long as we have, what with long-distance telephone calls, and Bray driving truckloads of furniture out here all the time and buying up all the material in downtown Perdido so Lucille can sew dresses. We can't keep it secret forever, and besides we wouldn't want to. We'd want the two of you and Tommy Lee to come see us, too. So what are we supposed to say when people come up to us and say, 'That's a precious little baby boy! What cloud did *he* drop out of?'"

"I don't suppose you'd want to say you were raped at Lake Pinchona," said Queenie.

"Shhhh!" said Grace. "Of course not."

"We could say she got married, and that's why she went off," suggested James. "And we could say her boyfriend got killed in the war. And then she found out she was pregnant and this is her little boy. We could say that."

"That's a good story," said Lucille. "People would believe that."

And so they did.

Eventually, Frances and Miriam were admitted to the family confidence and told the truth. Frances was taken completely by surprise, but know-it-all Miriam said, "I would have had to be blind, deaf, and stupid not to have figured the whole thing out."

"Why didn't you say you knew, then?" said Sister, dubious.

"It wasn't any of my business," returned Miriam. "I just hope nobody expects me to go out there and see them, that's all."

"Why not?" said James.

"Because my idea of a good time is not a stagnant pond that breeds mosquitoes and a house that's filled with bugs and a baby crying in the next room, that's why."

"It's real pleasant out at the pond," said James in mild reproof, "and Tommy Lee is the sweetest baby I have ever laid eyes on. I'm gone make Bray drive me out there every day."

"You cain't do that, James," said Queenie peremptorily. "Those two girls want to be alone with their baby. I never saw two people happier together. They don't want you and me bouncing in on 'em every morning, noon, and night."

Learning about the situation, Billy Bronze was able to help. He surreptitiously went through some files at Eglin and found the name of a boy who had been at the base at the time of the rape, and who had subsequently died in the South Pacific. His name was LeRoy Burgess, and he had no next-of-kin. LeRoy Burgess became the posthumous husband of Lucille and the father of Tommy Lee.

On the first of July, 1944, Lucille's child was christened Tommy Lee Burgess in the First Methodist Church of Perdido, with the boy's mother and Grace standing together at the baptismal font. There was a little reception at Elinor's afterward, and if Perdido didn't believe the story the Caskeys told, Perdido at least had the courtesy not to say so. Grace said to everyone, "Soon as Tommy Lee is old enough, Lucille and I are gone toss him in the back seat and drive out to Oklahoma and buy us some Black Angus heifers. Nothing takes to a pecan pasture like a Black Angus..."

CHAPTER 56

Lazarus

Even though Germany hadn't surrendered to the Allies, the war seemed to be winding down. Perdido felt it because the nearby air base felt it. Teenage boys were still being trained and sent off to Europe and to the Pacific, but one could sense that things had changed; unmistakably, the war was coming to an end. Orders for lumber, posts, and window sashes continued to pour in, however, and the Caskeys' prosperity gave no sign of slackening. Miriam worked ever more closely with her father at the mill; the workers had long before grown accustomed to seeing her there. She was no longer simply Mr. Oscar's girl, she was Miss Miriam, and respected in her own right.

The operation of the Caskey mill was in two parts. The exterior portion included the mill-yard with all its machinery, workers, and storage facilities as well as the forests and the vehicles and other means by which the lumber was transported. The interior portion consisted of the offices in the center of the mill-yard, the workers in the office, the files, the paper-work, the hired accountants and lawyers, and the dealings with customers. That the sole customer at this time continued to be the United States War Department made the running of the concern no eas-ier.

In her three years there, Miriam had nearly taken over the entire internal operation of the mill. Even Elinor, who somehow managed to keep close tabs on the mill without ever setting foot within its bound-aries, knew that Miriam had accomplished this not through subtle maneuverings against her father and over the heads of the employees, but completely through her own competence and energy. Because Oscar was so often off somewhere in the forest, or attending to some piece of business out of town, em-ployees had gone to Miriam with their problems in-stead of to Oscar. Miriam's sensible and sound replies, commands, and advice were always seconded by her father upon his return. Miriam soon became more than simply Oscar's representative; he came more and more to rely upon his daughter in the routine matters of the running of the mill. He built her an office next to his, and he gave her her own secretary and telephone line. Calls from the outside were routed automatically to her now. She was as decisive in all her dealings as any man in Perdido might have been in her place. She worked longer hours than her father, but it was in fact her dedication to the mill that allowed Oscar to take a little ease after so many years of unrelieved toil.

Considering the early hostilities that had sepa-rated Miriam from her parents for so many years, Oscar and Miriam were more intimate than anyone in Perdido would ever have thought possible. Theirs was not the intimacy of a father with his daughter, but that of a proud businessman with his promising young partner. After breakfast in the morning, Oscar went next door for a second cup of coffee with Miriam before Bray drove them to the mill together. Sister left the room, knowing that they would talk only business. Bray brought them home at noon, and for a brief time they were part of the larger Caskey family, and refrained from speaking of the mill, except in general terms. After lunch, Miriam returned to the mill while her father lingered at home or drove out into the Caskey forests or went on business to Eglin, Pensacola, or Mobile. After supper, Oscar and Miriam sometimes went off together, sitting on Miriam's side porch or walking together out behind the houses, talking of the mill and the infinite minutiae of the business.

Though she became accustomed to spending a great deal of time with her father, Miriam had no more to do with her mother than she'd had all her life. A great distance remained between them; Miriam was close only to her father. When younger, this distance had shown itself in silence, in her solitude, in her constant cold-shouldering. Now, when she was so often thrown in with her family, such methods would not do. She instead relied on an abruptness of manner, a curtness of speech, an aloof expression, and a general lack of interest in the family good unless it was consistent with the good of the Caskey mills. This harshness was accepted by Miriam's family, just as every other aberration was accepted by the Caskeys. No one sought to change her, no one considered that she would be better off if she softened her ways. Elinor once said, "That's the way Miriam is. Everybody ought to be grateful that she'll sit at the same table with us." There had been some sotto voce complaints in the town and among the mill workers—among those who did not really know Miriam—about a young woman's being given so much power and responsibility, but Oscar Caskey never considered reining in his daughter's ambition. All in the family were proud of her for what she was doing. It was no more peculiar for Miriam to want to work ten hours day at a desk in the dusty mill-yard, with nothing to see out her window but stacks of lumber and nothing to hear but the chippers and the saws, than for Grace and Lucille to want to live out at Gavin Pond and sleep in the same narrow bed with a one-year-old boy and two smelly bird dogs.

Miriam appeared hard and peremptory to those who worked in the office of the mill, but to her family she had definitely softened. She had grown up a child indulged in every conceivable way by her grandmother Mary-Love, and after Mary-Love's death Sister had done nothing to keep Miriam from pursuing that same aimless, self-indulgent way of life. Working at the mill, being compelled to deal with customers and subordinates, and maintaining a relationship with her father—a relationship that did have at least a casual intimacy—had smoothed some of Miriam's rougher edges. She was compelled to think of others, to figure out motives for behavior, determine prejudices, and try to understand nuances of behavior. Her churlishness now was a choice, not a deficiency of her basic personality.

Indicative of this new sensitivity in Miriam was the way that she now treated Sister Haskew. During the war, Sister, now in her early fifties, had become what everyone had always said she would turn out to be—a spinster. She forgot, as nearly as it was possible to forget, that she ever had had a husband. Early Haskew had been in California, Michigan, Greece, England, and France. He had sent Sister postcards from each of those places, and Sister—after always glancing at the postmarks—had torn them up, unread. She shuddered as she ripped the cards in two: "I don't even want to *think* about that man."

"Why don't you get a divorce?" asked Miriam one

morning at breakfast after Ivey had brought in one of the cards. This one had a photograph of the Roman Coliseum on it.

"Nobody in this family has ever gotten a divorce," said Sister.

"You could be the first."

Sister looked at Miriam strangely. "What would I get a divorce *for*? Early's never *done* anything to me."

"Then why don't you ever want to see him again?"

"You shouldn't ask me that question."

"Why not?"

Sister paused. "Because I don't know the answer."

Miriam picked up the scraps of the postcard, and dropped them one by one onto her plate. She said, "The reason you married Early was to spite Grandmama."

Sister nodded.

"But after Grandmama died, there was no reason to stay married to Early. Early chews tobacco."

"He made me feed his dogs out of a nipple-bottle. Twice a night, I had to get up and feed those puppies. It was like having six children all at once. He put a Coke machine on the front porch of our house." Sister blushed with the memory. "I came home one day and saw that, and I said, 'If Mama were to come up here and see this, I would have to lay down in the road and die of shame.'"

"And that's why, when Mama died, you stayed on here. You didn't stay to keep care of me, you stayed 'cause you didn't want to go back to Early."

"How long have you known this?"

"I just this minute figured it out," said Miriam with a little shrug.

"I loved you, darling, and I *did* want to take care of you."

"I know you did, Sister."

"You don't want me to go back to Early, do you?

169

I know you could get along fine without me, and I know this house really and truly belongs to you, but I don't want to go back to Nashville or wherever it is that man is living now. Miriam, darling, sometimes I sit up in my room at night, and I think, 'What if Miriam gets married and she moves her husband in here, is she gone throw me out?' Would you do that, would you throw me out?"

"Sister, you're rich, don't you know that? Grandmama left all her money to you and Oscar. All I got was this house and the safety-deposit boxes. If I threw you out of here, you could go anywhere you wanted to. You could set up housekeeping in the main street of New Orleans if you wanted to. If you wanted to stay in Perdido, you could get the DeBordenave house from James and fix it all up any way you liked it."

"That's not answering my question."

Miriam grinned. "I'm not gone get married. I haven't got time. I'm working every minute of the day and half the night. And even if I did," she added in a lower voice, "I'd never throw you out."

"That's what I wanted to hear!"

"Are you satisfied?" said Miriam, rising from the table. "Where do you suppose Oscar is? It's getting late."

"Miriam, come hug me!"

"What for?"

"For being so sweet!"

"Oh, Sister, whoever called me sweet before?"

"Well, I never did—and nobody else did either, within *my* hearing. But we were all wrong—every one of us."

Miriam went over and put her arms briefly about Sister's neck. Sister reached up and squeezed Miriam's clenched fists as hard as she could.

All James Caskey's prayers and all Billy Bronze's words in the ear of his commanding officer had not

been able to keep Danjo Strickland from being transferred away from Eglin Air Base.

"This is going to kill me," said James to his nephew
when Danjo told him of the orders.

"It is not," said Danjo. "By the time I get over
there, wherever it is they're sending me, the war is
gone be over."

"Who's gone die first?" demanded James Caskey
querulously. "You or me? Are you gone get shot before I die of grief? Or I am gone get laid out in my
casket before you get mown down on the battlefield?"

"Neither one is gone happen," said Danjo calmly.
"That's why I was trained in radio. They don't put
their radiomen at the front. Or at least most of 'em
stay way behind the lines. Besides, look at Germany
right now, where are there lines? We're beating 'em
way back, James."

James rocked violently on the porch and wouldn't
look up at Danjo, as if somehow all this were his
doing.

"Hey, look at me, James."

James looked up but didn't stop rocking.

"I don't want to go," said Danjo softly. "I don't
want to leave you. Don't you think I'm gone miss
you?"

"Don't bother to write," said James.

"Why not?"

" 'Cause I'm gone be dead."

Two days after Danjo was shipped out, Germany
surrendered. James was certain that Danjo therefore
was being sent to the continued, bloody fighting in
the Pacific.

Billy heard two weeks later that Danjo was in
Germany, billeted in a castle on a mountaintop east
of Munich. His sole duty was to signal Allied planes
a safe path to a nearby landing field.

A letter confirming this arrived a few days later.

Danjo complained of nothing but the boredom and the strict injunction against the fraternizing with the conquered citizenry. The castle had its own cook, its own farm, even its own vineyard. The graf and his two daughters lived in rooms below his. The graf was a nice old man who reminded Danjo of James— except, of course, the graf didn't speak English and didn't like Americans—and the two daughters were very pretty and very nice and made his bed for him every morning.

Billy heard this letter read aloud at the dinner table. He sighed and said, "Let him complain. When I think of the number of men I trained who're dead now..."

"He could fall off that mountain," said James. "That old graf could murder him in his bed!" James had somehow got it into his head that "graf" meant "cobbler," and he wondered how a shoemaker came into possession of a castle.

"Nothing's going to happen to Danjo," said Queenie sternly. "James, I don't want you to imagine one single thing more."

James was seventy-five. It had been his lifelong quirk to show his age only in fits and starts. He would go along for five, ten, or fifteen years with no perceptible alteration of appearance or demeanor. Then one single event would suddenly pour down those years upon his head in a single moment. Such had been the case when his wife Genevieve had died violently on the Atmore road; he had then been a well-preserved young man suddenly thrust into middle years. The death of his sister-in-law Mary-Love had swept the well-preserved middle-aged man into old age. This departure of Danjo to Europe pitched James Caskey from a sturdy old age into incipient senility.

James was alone and Queenie was alone, so Queenie gave up her house and moved in with James.

172

She even laughed about the situation to Elinor: "When I came to Perdido twenty-something years ago, I thought to myself, 'I'll get a divorce from Carl and then I'll marry James Caskey. He's a rich man and his money will make me happy.' That seemed real simple. Now it's hard to even think of all the things that have happened over those years. But here I am, moving in with him, and it's *me* that's taking care of *him*. And you know what's real funny, Elinor?"

"What?"

"That I don't even *think* about money anymore." Queenie let out a little ironic chuckle.

Two or three times a week Queenie drove James out to Gavin Pond to visit their daughters. James loved the infant Tommy Lee and held him on his lap for as long as Tommy Lee would allow it. But James couldn't always remember the boy's name, and called him variously Danjo, Malcolm, and John Robert. James often seemed to have forgotten all about Danjo, and listened only vacantly to the letters that Queenie read to him. At the end of them, James would always say impatiently, "Queenie, let's go out to the pond this afternoon. I need a little boy on my lap."

"We were there yesterday, James," Queenie would sometimes have to say.

"Yesterday?"

"That's right. And we cain't go again today, those girls would get tired of us and put a padlock on that gate."

Sometimes at night Queenie would be awakened by the sound of James stumbling through the darkened house. He'd push open the door of her room and stand as Lazarus might have stood, bewildered at the mouth of the tomb. His wide-open eyes saw nothing.

"Who's in here?" he'd call into the darkness. "Grace, is that you? Genevieve?"

"It's me—Queenie. James, go back to bed."

"Where is everybody? Why is the house empty?"

CHAPTER 57

The Flight

The death of President Franklin D. Roosevelt in April, 1945, made a greater impression on Perdido than had the bombing of Pearl Harbor or the other great events of World War II. Roosevelt, after all, had been talked of daily for more than a dozen years. All the church bells in town had rung out for half an hour on D-Day. They rang out twice that long to mourn the death of the president. The German surrender soon afterward made a smaller impression.

Frances and Billy Bronze had made no definite plans to be wed, but the death of Roosevelt and the end of fighting in Europe made everyone feel, justifiably or not, that the war was over. Discipline at Eglin was more relaxed than ever. Enlisted men wanted only to go to the beach and stretch out their time in Billy's classes until the day of the Japanese surrender, which surely could not be far off. On the screened porch upstairs one day after lunch, Billy

Bronze said to Elinor, "Maybe Frances and I should think about July."

"Are you getting out of the service?" asked Elinor.

"I've already started on that. I've been in a long time and I think they'll let me go."

Elinor eyed her future son-in-law with humorous mistrust. "You haven't been changing your mind, have you?"

"About what, Mrs. Caskey?"

"About taking my little girl away from me. She's all I've got."

Billy laughed. That Elinor Caskey, head of her family, rich, always surrounded with relatives, sought after in the town and known even in Mobile and Pensacola, should declare that her younger daughter was all that she had, seemed ridiculous to Billy.

"It's true," said Elinor seriously. "If you were to take Frances away, it would kill me. And what's more, it would kill Frances, too."

"I don't believe that," said Billy. "But I'm not taking her away, so there's nothing to worry about."

"I'm glad to hear it," said Elinor. "There's plenty of room in this house for all of us."

"Yes, ma'am," returned Billy. "I just hope you and Mr. Caskey are prepared to support a son-in-law for a while. My daddy's got all the money in the world, but I'm not going to see a crying dime of it before he dies. And it may be some time before I can even find a job."

"We're not worried," Elinor reassured him. "We'll let you know when to stop taking advantage of us."

Billy was released from the Air Corps during the first week in July. All his belongings had been moved into Oscar and Elinor's house. He and Frances were married late in the month in a simple ceremony in the sweltering heat of Elinor's living room. No one

176

in Perdido could understand why the Caskeys, rich as they were, never went in for large church weddings, as anyone else in their position assuredly would have done. Elinor Caskey could certainly have afforded a splendid wedding for her daughter, but the whole ceremony and reception probably had cost her less than fifty dollars. Perhaps, Perdido considered, Frances was pregnant. The truth was that the Caskeys were only following their custom. Their weddings were always sudden, hasty, casual affairs. Not one of them would have felt comfortable seeing the bride in a church, with mounds of flowers and rows of bridesmaids. There was also the difficulty of Billy's father, who had refused to attend, to send congratulations, to speak to any member of the bride's family over the telephone, or even to contribute five dollars as a wedding gift. At the end of the ceremony, before Billy and Frances had even broken their first wedded embrace, Miriam flung aside her wilting bouquet and cried, "Good Lord! Come on upstairs, Sister, and help me get out of this damned dress. There's a pin been sticking in my side since two o'clock!"

Billy and Frances were pleased by the modestness of the wedding. It seemed more in keeping with the tenor of their quiet courtship than anything larger would have been. They honeymooned in New Orleans for a week, and returned directly to Perdido. Although Billy's possessions were stored in the front room, the couple slept in Frances's room next to the sleeping porch.

The Caskeys were satisfied with Frances's new husband. One day not long after the wedding, Elinor said to Sister and to Queenie, "Do you notice a little bit of a difference between Mary-Love and me? Do you notice that my little girl got married, but is not leaving home? Do you see that her husband is perfectly content to live under my roof?"

Miriam, though she said nothing, was grateful to Billy for not seeking a job at the mill, where her carefully built-up power would have been threatened by the force of his authority as a man.

With money supplied her by her father, Grace Caskey was able to buy up approximately five thousand acres of farming land around and contiguous to Gavin Pond. Most of it had been fallow since the beginning of the Depression, and some of it was nearly subtropical forest, with alligator ponds and creeks that flowed so smoothly and quietly that they seemed not to flow at all. Grace didn't want yet to put this land to use, but like all the other Caskeys, she felt better just *owning* it. Now she knew no one would invade her and Lucille's cherished privacy. Their remoteness was insured.

Grace lured Luvadia Sapp out to live at Gavin Pond with a promise of unlimited fishing rights. Luvadia brought with her her three-year-old illegitimate son Sammy, fathered by Roxie's forty-three-year-old son Escue. They lived in the kitchen for six weeks or so until Escue Welles built them a little house of their own, hidden in the cypress grove across the pond and next to the graveyard. Luvadia could see the epitaphs out her kitchen window. Escue decided not to return to Perdido, but to remain with Luvadia and Sammy. He gave up his job at the mill and was hired by Grace as her overseer. Escue knew less about farming than anyone Grace had ever met, but he was a hard worker and Luvadia loved him.

Grace had cleared out the pecan orchard the spring before, cutting out the oak and pine saplings that had destroyed the symmetry of the grid of massive trees. She had mown the grass short, and cleared out the stream that ran through it. With Lucille she had gone to Miami, Oklahoma, and bought seventy-five heifers. Even Lucille could tell the cows apart, and she kept careful records of their pedigrees, especially after the acquisition of Zato, their prize bull, worth every penny of the eleven thousand dollars that was paid for him. The animals had grazed contentedly among the pecan trees all summer long, but autumn had come now, and Grace was looking forward to the harvest of the nuts.

One morning late in September 1945, just before dawn, Grace climbed into her pickup truck and took off for Babylon. Luvadia and Escue sat together in the back of the vehicle. Grace drove into the colored section of town and started blowing her horn. Luvadia and Escue stood up on the bed of the truck, and shouted, "Pecans! Pecans!"

Grace drove slowly. Teenage boys and girls flew off their front porches and out of their yards and leaped onto the back of the truck. In the houses, unemployed men were roused out of their sleep by their wives, shoved into their clothes, and pushed out the door toward the truck. Mothers climbed up with their babies wrapped in slings around their necks. Grace stopped occasionally for an old decrepit woman to be hoisted up with the rest. When the back of the truck could hold no more, Grace took off down the road toward Gavin Pond.

At the gate of the pecan orchard, each picker was given a croker sack to fill. Luvadia took all the children too young to work over to her house and set them on the floor with Sammy. The black workers fairly flew at the trees and began picking up all the nuts on the ground. Grace, armed with a large stick, patrolled for snakes and shooed away the curious cows. The two biggest black men went systematically down each row of the orchard, threw their arms about the trunk of each tree—the circumference of which always surpassed the reach of their arms— and shook it until the pecans showered down.

The pickers worked all morning, forever stooped, never looking up, sometimes singing hymns to-

179

gether, sometimes only humming to themselves, sometimes scolding the children or trading gossip. Lucille and Luvadia brought out innumerable plates of biscuits and cornbread, and one child did nothing but fill jugs of water at the stream that flowed through the orchard.

They stopped at eleven and went to Luvadia's house where they were all served ham and black-eyed peas and collard greens. Grace and Lucille themselves dished up and passed out plates. The pecan gatherers agreed, when they returned to their work that afternoon, that no farmers had ever been so kind to them. During the day the workers dragged their croker sacks—either filled or too heavy to work with anymore—up to the porch of the house. There they were weighed by Escue, and tallies kept beside the names of the pickers. At three o'clock Grace totalled the weights and paid out to the pickers at the rate of five cents a pound. Some earned as much as six or seven dollars. Afterward she drove them all back to Babylon. Many fell asleep immediately upon climbing onto the bed of the truck, despite the bumpiness of the ride through the forest. They all hopped out in the center of the colored section of town, and Grace promised that she would be back bright and early the following morning.

News got around that night in Babylon, and next morning Grace didn't even have to blow her horn. Colored people were waiting on their front porches in every direction, and she made only a single stop. The back of the truck was filled instantly. Luvadia and Escue even sat up front with Grace so that a few more could be crowded into the back. So many were disappointed that Grace promised to make a return trip that morning.

For two weeks the pickers came to Gavin Pond, and at the end of that time there was not a single pecan left on the ground or in the trees. Grace gave each of her pickers a two-dollar bonus for having been so thorough. The living room of the house was filled with croker sacks of pecans. With Escue's help Grace loaded the sacks into the truck and carried them to the pecan wholesaler in Jay and received twenty cents a pound. She saved a sack for herself, a second sack for Luvadia, and took four more to Perdido. Miriam requisitioned two of the sacks, divided the pecans into ten-pound lots, and mailed them to purchasing agents in the North.

Grace's seven-hundred-dollar profit was modest, and it wouldn't begin to pay back what she had spent on heifers or the purchase of land or the improvements she had been making on the property—but she was nonetheless proud of her work. She felt encouraged to go forward, and bought pigs and chickens. As soon as Tommy Lee was able to walk, he was given a small sack of grain and was taught by Sammy how to scatter food for the fowl.

The pecan harvest had a secondary effect, unforeseen by Grace and Lucille. It was their means of introduction to Babylon. Their existence was known throughout the black community, and eventually it came to be known in the white community as well. Grace realized that there was no longer any reason for keeping their existence secret, and began to trade at the grain and feed stores. A female farmer was not unknown in these parts, for there had been a tradition, following each of the wars, for widows to take over the running of the farms, and Grace commanded respect on several counts: her success with the pecan harvest, her purchase of so much land with ready cash, and her determined demeanor. Southerners are an easygoing race when it comes to aberrations of conduct. They will react with anger if something out of the ordinary is presented as a possible future occurrence; but if an unusual circumstance is discovered to be an established fact, they

181

will usually accept it without rancor or judgment as part of the normal order of things. To have informed the men who hung about the seed and feed stores that two women had bought Gavin Pond and were turning it into the biggest farm in the county would have brought out calls to repeal the voting rights amendment; but when confronted with Grace, the men were perfectly willing to accept her, her cousin Lucille, and Lucille's little boy.

The two women and the boy usually all drove into town together on Saturday, Grace at the wheel with Lucille beside her bouncing up and down on the seat with Tommy Lee on her lap. Luvadia, Escue, and Sammy were in the back. Everybody passing them on the road knew who they were and raised a single finger above the steering wheel in silent greeting. Grace and Escue shopped all Saturday afternoon, filling the back of the truck with grain and supplies, Luvadia and Sammy went to the grocery store and bought food for the coming week, and Lucille sat with Tommy Lee at the counter in the drugstore and gossiped. Grace and Lucille reflected on how different their life was here on the farm south of Babylon from what it had been in Perdido. The expectations of their youth had not been filled. Why on earth, Grace wondered, had she taught school when she was so much happier with her cows and pigs and chickens? How, thought Lucille, could she ever have flirted with those terrible servicemen when Grace had been so nearby?

Sometimes, during the week, Lucille left Tommy Lee with Luvadia, and she and Grace went into Babylon to eat a catfish supper and go to the picture show. This soon became a cherished habit with the cousins on Wednesday night, when the bill changed at the theater. People sitting on the front porches would point as the truck rattled by, and say, "There's Grace and Lucille on their way to the picture show. They probably don't even know what's playing."

Winter came to Gavin Pond. A few leaves turned brown, but the mild weather couldn't persuade them to drop off. Late summer flowers continued to bloom, determinedly ignoring the calendar. Sometimes Lucille and Grace put sweaters on when they went into town on Wednesday nights.

The second Wednesday in January 1946 was a cool evening. Leaving Tommy Lee in the charge of Luvadia, Grace and Lucille put on their sweaters, climbed into the truck, and drove into Babylon. They ate supper at the catfish place on the Ponce de Leon Road, where they were known to everyone, and where their usual meal was served without their ordering. Afterward, at the picture show, they saw a double bill of *Dillinger* and *Dangerous Partners*. They were out of the theater by eleven o'clock. The night was now even colder with bright stars. The waning moon would not rise till after midnight.

The Babylon post office closed its windows at five o'clock, but the front door was left open, allowing access to the boxes. Grace pulled up in front of the tiny brick building, went in the front door, walked over to the wall that the boxes were on, and twirled the combination. She pulled out a small sheaf of letters, slammed the little door shut, and returned to the truck.

"What did we get?" asked Lucille excitedly.

"Cattle auction ads for me, seed catalog for you, and a letter from Danjo."

"Oh, read it here!" Lucille switched on the light in the cab of the truck. After glancing at the German Occupation stamps on the envelope, Grace tore open the envelope and read:

Dear Grace,

I'm writing to you because I don't want to write

directly to James because he might get upset. The reason he might get upset is that I have just gotten myself married. That is wonderful and I know he'll be happy for me. The problem is she's German and I can't get her out of the country yet. I wasn't even supposed to meet her, regulations against fraternization with the enemy and all that, but I did, and we fell in love. She is the graf's daughter who owns this castle, his oldest daughter. The graf died last month so we got married. Her name is Fredericka von Hoeringmeister. I call her Fred, so now she is Fred Strickland. She doesn't have any money and it takes a lot of money to keep up a castle, so she will probably let her sister have it and we will come back to Alabama. That is, as soon as I can arrange to get her out. She wasn't a Nazi or anything. The graf wasn't either. But he still didn't like Americans and that's why Fred and I waited until he was dead. Does Oscar know anybody in Congress? Congress could help me get Fred back to Alabama. I don't know what to do about James. Should I write to him? Will you talk to him? Fred doesn't mind living with him when we come back, if he doesn't mind having a German in the house. Fred made my bed every morning, that's how I met her. There were about fifteen of us occupying the castle. I'll be out of the Air Corps in six months, then I'll try to come back. But I won't come back unless I can bring Fred with me. I'm going to leave all this up to you, Grace. You tell everybody. I can't be writing ten letters all saying the same thing.

Sincerely yours,
Danjo

P.S. Fred says "hi."

This letter was surprising, and the object of discussion between Grace and Lucille all the way back to Gavin Pond. Grace dreaded telling her father not only that his precious boy was married, but that because of that marriage, he might be delayed in his long-awaited return to Perdido.

"Cain't help it, though," argued Lucille. "James's got to find out. We cain't keep this thing secret from the whole family. And if one of them finds out, it's bound to get back to James, so you might as well tell him straight off. He'll get over it, especially if Danjo says he's coming back, and he and Fred will stay in the house with James. I wonder what she's like. I hope he's taught her to speak English."

"Well," said Grace, turning off the dark road into the even darker forest, "I'm not gone make any decisions in the middle of the night. Let's us decide in the morning."

Grace drove slowly. The truck jolted over the hard ground. Grace leaned over the steering wheel and peered into the night. Lucille bounced up and down and held her pocketbook over her head to keep from getting hurt when she bounced against the roof of the cab.

When they reached the gate to the farm, Lucille got out and pushed it open. Grace drove the truck through, and Lucille jumped on the running board for the short quarter mile to the house.

No lights shone inside the house. "Luvadia must have fallen asleep again," said Lucille, shaking her head as she jumped down from the running board.

Grace turned off the ignition, and cried, "No! Listen!"

From inside the house—through the open window of their own bedroom—they heard a faint, masculine voice, singing.

"Who in the world—" began Lucille.

"It's Daddy," whispered Grace in wonder. She opened the door of the truck quietly, and got out.

185

"What in the world is James doing out here this time of night?" said Lucille. "And where is his car?"

Grace shook her head. She shivered. The evening was suddenly very cold.

"What's he doing up there?" said Lucille, and came around the truck, taking hold of Grace's hand. They stared up at the darkened bedroom window.

"He's singing to Tommy Lee," said Grace quietly. "Shhh! Lord! I had forgot that song, he used to sing it to me every night. It's a lullaby."

James Caskey's voice, tremulous and faint, floated out of the window.

> "Fly, ladybird, fly
> Your daddy's hanging high
> Your mama's shut in Moscow town
> Moscow town is burning down
> Fly, ladybird, fly"

At the end of the song, his voice drifted off. All the world seemed silent. In the darkness Lucille and Grace looked at each other, and then they quietly went into the house through the kitchen. They found Luvadia sitting at the table, with her head on her crossed arms, sleeping.

Grace gently shook her awake.

"Miss Grace," said Luvadia groggily, even before she had opened her eyes.

"When did Daddy get out here?" Grace asked.

"Ma'am?"

"Daddy?" Grace repeated. "When did Daddy get here?"

"Ma'am? Mr. James not here..."

Lucille was already at the bottom of the stairs with her foot on the lowest step.

Grace hurried after her. "No," she cried, "don't go up!"

"Tommy Lee..." said Lucille in explanation, and began to mount the stairs to the darkened bedroom.

Grace pushed past Lucille and hurried to the second floor. She flung open the door of the bedroom. A violent gust of wind blew through the room, and the curtains were flung with a *whoosh* out into the night air.

Grace ran to the bassinet, but even in the darkness she knew that Tommy Lee was no longer there.

She ran to the window, threw her head out, and shouted, "Daddy! Bring him back!"

The light came on in the room behind her.

Lucille said, "Grace! What in the world—"

Grace turned around with agony in her face.

Tommy Lee lay sleeping on the bed, cradled between two pillows. Beside the sleeping infant was a long indentation in the soft mattress, outlining a human form.

Wonderingly, Lucille ran her hand over that depression in the chenille spread. "It's still warm," she said.

Downstairs, the telephone rang. Grace snatched Tommy Lee up from the bed and cradled him in her arms. "You go get it," said Grace.

Glancing back at the tears in Grace's eyes, Lucille ran down the stairs.

It was Queenie calling, to say that James had had a heart attack and was dead. "I came in just now," said Queenie, in a wandering, distracted voice, "and I found him lying right across the living room door. If I hadn't turned on the light first, I would have tripped right over him."

SIX MONTHS OF
BLOODCURDLING
HORROR

MICHAEL McDOWELL'S
CONTINUING SAGA OF THE CASKEY FAMILY.

BLACKWATER

BLACKWATER, an epic novel of horror, will appear serially for six months beginning in January 1983 with completion in June. Michael McDowell, described by Stephen King as "the finest writer of paperback originals in America," is at the height of his storytelling prowess as he tells of the powers exerted by the mysterious Elinor Dammert over the citizens of Perdido, Alabama. Her ghastly, inexplicable ability to use water to gain her hideous ends is a recurring and mystifying pattern.

> ## "Michael McDowell's best book yet...He is one of the best writers of horror in this country."
> ### -Peter Straub

This multi-generational occult thriller takes place from 1919 to the 1980s, with horrendous and chilling occurrences in each volume. The terror will mount from month to month in the six volumes of this epic novel, which will be on sale as follows:

THE FLOOD (January)

THE LEVEE (February)

THE HOUSE (March)

THE WAR (April)

THE FORTUNE (May)

RAIN (June)

Avon Paperbacks